Death Listens Not to Me

~ of the Old Ways ~

C. N. Eisenbruch

This text contains the following elements that may induce a trauma response in readers:

- Self-harm
- Mentions of suicide
- Suicidal ideation

If you or someone you know is in crisis, please call, text or chat with the Suicide and Crisis Lifeline at 988, or contact the Crisis Text Line by texting TALK to 741741.

---

*"Now watch me laugh
as I burn
all the memories
of
you."*

- Joey Batey with Joe Trapanese, *Burn Butcher Burn*

Table Of Contents

Chapter I............A Beginning 1

Chapter II ....Funeral Rites 18

Chapter III ....A Once Great King...28

Chapter IV ....Love Struck, Blood Suck 43

Chapter V ....Beltane 85

Chapter VI.........Spear Of The Hunt...72

Chapter VII.........Dragon's Scale 86

Chapter VIII ....Wolves At Bay...100

Chapter IX ....Bless The Rains 115

Chapter X............Where Tread The Gods 133

Chapter XI ....The Legendary Chymera 154

Chapter XII.........To War...169

Chapter XIII ....Dread Plague 186

Chapter XIV ....The Pursuit Of Gainne And Diarmuid ...202

Chapter XV.........Holy Priests Of Bjirtka....................................221

Chapter XVI ....An End..237

I

A BEGINNING

Bubbles of gore pool in the corners of lips that move soundlessly. The crunch of his victim's bones from a slice of his sword drown out the dying man's final words. As the warrior stands, clutching the superficial wounds left him by his opponents, he waits. And he listens.

How long have I been doing this?

A man charged him, face contorted into a snarl; something between rage and confidence written in its lines. Mottled brown hair stuck to a bleeding wound that seemed to fall only too lightly upon his brow, giving the man a second chance to run from a battle he had no chance of winning. Yet there it was: the same self-serving sense of purpose he'd seen in all their faces just before they fell. Angry, determined, filled with a twisted sense of pride and arrogance. They were sure they would send him to the goddess, sure they would reap whatever glory came with his death.

They did not understand her ways.

The shield began to lower and the axe came up high, rising behind him. A waste of movement, too great a lowering of his guard. It wouldn't do to fall to such an unworthy effort. It would be inglorious to succumb to an attack he could see had no business reaching him. He ducked low as the enraged man drew close enough to strike, launching a shoulder tackle into his knees.

Using the man's momentum to flip him across his back, the warrior left him to fall headfirst into the rocky soil beneath him. His opponent gasped, pain and shock in the labored breath that marked his last. The warrior's sword went cleanly into his opponent's exposed neck, leaving his body to sink lifeless to the earth.

I'm so tired of this.

But there was no rest. Another man, a smearing of pitch and muck obscuring the expression already enmeshed in a scraggly black beard, closed upon him with a winged spear. The tip extended a bit too far - cautiously, it seemed to the warrior. He'd been quiet in his approach but now lunged forward. Leaving his feet planted awkwardly and legs strained into a position too upright for the attack, his lower half appeared as though it resisted the advance toward which his upper half reached.

How is it she prefers the likes of you? He seethed in his mind.

He caught the spear by the shaft in his left hand, the slow, awkward attack giving him ample time. Just as he did, he stepped backward into a low lunge, jerking the man forward. Sword slices cleanly through ribs as he trips, torn off balance by the warrior's stronger grasp upon his spear.

You should be so lucky, to stumble into her embrace. Bastard.

The blade passes too deeply for recovery into his opponent's body and he abandoned it within him, the hilt pressed into the ground beneath the weight of the corpse. The warrior was unfazed. The spear he'd caught would serve just as well, perhaps even more so. He favored no weapon over another. In fact, the less familiar it was to him, the better. He could extend himself fully and perhaps still be so fortunate as to find the gap in his ability. He could hope for that flaw's exploitation. He could hope that another might cut him down.

Through the mud and the whispering rain, he could see the folk around him that had endeavored to form a pitiful semblance of a militia. They held weapons. Some even bore armor. Yet none were warriors. The bandits they faced were fewer in number but outmatched them terribly in experience and ferocity. Holding a weapon didn't make one able to fight, nor did wearing armor make one invulnerable. He'd seen it all too often as he wrought his own fine work for too many ultimately unworthy clients. Ironic that the Morrigan should wash their armor even before they first donned it.

Ironic, and unjust, He thought with a grimace.

He would not let them go to her embrace before him. He would not let these ordinary folk meet a bloody end, would not see them dine and take respite before her hearth for having held a weapon but once in a futile effort to frighten off creatures that had no reason to cower before them.

No. Better the bandits than them.

The warrior had slowed the advance of the attacking force, but the paltry defense proved too tempting for them to retreat. They avoided him, knowing that he was no trifling prey, but still sought to press the attack against these weaker foes. Villagers, farmers, who fought with the tenacity of they who would defend their homeland with their last drop of blood and final gasp of breath.

Fools. Do they truly understand so little?

He practically leapt from man to man, skewering them as they sought to fall upon those common folk, cowering behind swords and spears and shields their bodies scarcely could bear the weight of.

None of you deserve this.

He washed across the field like a wave. By the time a man met their death on the end of his spear he had already begun an attack upon the next. His company rallied their morale, awestruck and terrified that such a warrior had been among them, confounded by his movements and convinced of some greater righteousness in his heart. They could not understand the truth behind his actions.

For he acted only to play her sweet song. To draw forth the rapture and the melody of the Morrigan - Goddess of Death, and Chooser of the slain in battle.

The cacophony of clattering weapons and bloodied, gurgling breaths spread across the field, each adding but a few small notes before falling silent. The "music" followed and surrounded him, until finally, new notes rang out. They were fleeing from the battle, calling their retreat while his would-be comrades hollered, vocalizing their perceived victory. The warrior spat a curse and looked about frantically, caught in the frenzy of adrenaline and a melancholy desperation unique to the obsessed, born of yearning and jealousy.

No black feathers fell upon him. No otherworldly voice called, no vision of his beloved met him. He saw them fleeing into the wood instead, heard their footfalls and shouting. He could not see her; he wanted to see her.

I will meet her. I will meet her this very day.

So he gave chase, hurling the spear he'd been using
too well into the thigh of a fleeing man, calling for the
frightened bandit and his fellows to return and face him.
To stand as men and fight with honor. Empty words, and
an empty plea. A ruse to persuade them to play the odds
against a single man to an end that would favor them.
Rage possesses men to act in ways they know better than
to behave. Fools in love are much the same.

He took up the dropped sword of the man whose thigh
his spear soundly impaled, paying him no further mind.
He needed someone better to lure her to him, he believed.
This man would die a frightened coward, caught running
with his back to his foe.

Worthless.

But his voice did carry to a number of the other bandits,
who quickly realized that the enemy "force" was now
but a single man. It seemed to them that the only natural
course was to have their revenge against the lone warrior.
The calculation was easy enough to make; four ought to
best one.

See me. Take me. Hear my prayer, goddess.

Despite his prayers, four was not enough to best this one.

The warrior had brought many to the Morrigan, seeking
to find her on his own yet always evaded by this most
fickle of mistresses. In vain does he wait for her call. In
vain does he plead for her blessing.

If you will not find me, I will seek you myself.

They are dead around him. Their swords are not enough

to claim his life. In vain does he take matters into his own hands, attempt to carve his own path through the dagger plunged into his belly.

She is deaf to his prayers. She rejects his offering.

—

He awoke upon a slab of stone not uncomfortably done up with straw and furs. As he grew more aware of his surroundings he could feel the bandage wound tightly around his torso. Breathing brought the sensation of stitches tugging at the edges of the wound in his gut. *Not an easy operation*, he noted to himself; *yet I still live.*

A figure moves across his vision. An ample form bearing the simple woolen robes of a priestess tended to the smokey peat fire burning cheerfully in the hearth. Through the dim light he can make out her uncovered auburn hair and the runes embroidered along the sleeves and collar of her tunic, marking both her maidenhood and her status as high priestess. *No mere hedge witch, then,* he thinks. Considering her medicinal prowess it fit. She turns to regard him.

"Ah, you're awake. Lucky that. A more skilled swordsman would be in a much less comfortable bed." She speaks in a soft, but clear voice, one used to being acknowledged as an authority and unused to being challenged. She draws back the furs to check his dressings, then tucks them back in place once she's satisfied he's not bled through the bandages.

"You're tougher than you look, that's for certain, but I don't recommend moving."

He exhaled slowly, not knowing how to admit the

comfort of the bed and warmth of the fire meant he wasn't going anywhere. He coughed, testing his voice.

"May I know with whom I speak?"

She studied him, the indigo of her eyes diving the icy blue depths of his own.

"No," she replied finally. "You're not actually interested, so there's no point."

She turns from him before her sentence is finished to a table set with linen and medicines, and so misses the comical myriad of expressions that crosses his face; not the least of which guilt at her speaking the truth, and annoyance that the truth seemed to affect her but little.

"On the contrary," he offered slowly, realizing he wasn't really in the best of positions to defend his wounded dignity. "Whether I want to thank you or not, I know that I should. And I am most grateful for the care that saved my life. I want only to give that caregiver a name, so I may thank her... properly."

"There's nothing proper about you, warrior. And I didn't ask to save your life, as much as you didn't want me to save it. From the looks of you, though," she said, turning back towards him and rubbing a callused finger along her chin thoughtfully as she studied the ink and skillful branding that marbled his pale flesh, similar in design to the embroidery on her own garments, "you should've known better than to attempt an offering you knew your goddess would reject."

Her words stung. He felt tears in the corners of his eyes. "You say you think the goddess... doesn't want me?"

His tone took much of the edge from her posture. She approached him slowly and knelt beside him, hands crossed over one another as though in prayer. "The Morrigan does not like to be told how to do her job. You come only when she calls you, and not a moment sooner."

He noticed, from the angle of her folded hands, deep scars that plunged across her wrists. She wore nothing to hide them, nor their kin who zigzagged up her arms like the stripes of a tiger.

"Now. Drink this," she said, uncorking a clay jug and holding up his head gently so he could both drink and breathe. The cordial's effects were near instantaneous. Before she'd even laid his head back down on the pillow he'd slipped from consciousness.

"I'm Qimmirea."

--

"They think you fell in battle, you know."

Her voice carried to him across the room again; this time a kitchen, and one he'd been able to slowly hobble around for some days now. She'd given him a bowl of potatoes to peel, and he wielded his dagger at that task as deftly as its more violent one.

"In battle? How so?"

"The man you slew. They found the rest of his band, and followed your trail of blood to each and every one of their corpses. Marauders, to the last man. You nearly died a hero's death, and all the village impatiently awaits for their humble priestess to deliver you up whole and healthy so they can celebrate your noble actions."

He cast a hooded glance over her, and the sly look she met him with matched her tone. "You get no hero's laurels then? For saving me?"

She shrugged and raised an eyebrow suggestively at the bowl of potatoes. "They pay me, what more should I expect?"

The warm peat fire's merry crackle kept the silence from hanging too heavily. Its light played in the furrows of his brow.

"What do you gain from hiding the truth?"

"What truth am I hiding? You *did* kill those men, and you *did* know they were bandits. Whether you did it in an attempt to end your own life is irrelevant, since they are dead and you are not."

"And... The Morrigan..." he trailed off and winced. As long as he'd been in the oratory, he'd come to realize just how devoutly this village worshipped their pagan deity. A hero rejected by their goddess should have no right to such a title. "She..."

"Like all self respecting deities, our holy Lady speaks not from her own mouth but through the mouths of her devout disciples. My word *is* the word of the Morrigan to these people."

The remainder of those words, though left unspoken, rang in the smoky kitchen chamber.

His life may be the least of what he owed her.

—

A brisk day on the brink of spring found the warrior crunching through rotting snow and snotty mud back up the winding hill. He often wondered whether it was Qimmirea's idea to have the oratory so far from the village, or the villagers'. Though every door in Eillear was open in hospitality to the wounded hero he still sought refuge with the priestess, often trudging back and forth between her oratory and the village. His professed reason was that of her healing prowess. He had yet to explore the unprofessed ones.

As he marched through the kitchen garden after a fairly prolonged absence, he noticed a table near the entrance haphazardly piled over with an assortment of random items.

"What is all that?" He asked curiously.

"Gifts," she replied dismissively, not taking her eyes from the altar.

"Gifts!! For the goddess, treated with such disdain?!" His voice rose in righteous anger. How dared she treat the deity and her worshippers so flippantly?

"Gifts for the *priestess*," she corrected, her dismissive tone becoming snooty.

He looked at the little *bean feasa*, as those who spoke the prophecies of the gods were called in those days, bowed over as she lit a row of candles. His eyebrow raised quizzically. "For you? Why would they bring you gifts?"

Despite the snootiness, she winced at that. "I haven't the faintest," she answered, and she stood up, blowing out the reed she'd used to light the altar. "But as a priestess who serves between a goddess and her worshippers, I've come to learn what gifts mean. They come with expectations, and wishes, that I've no right and no obligation to try to fulfill."

"So why keep them? Why take them at all?" He asked, arms crossed as he investigated the piles of flowers, rare treats, and candied fruits, among which more lavish tributes like ornate weapons and even jewels were sprinkled. "Just turn them down."

Shock finally managed to chase that dismissive and snooty tone from her voice. "Why, that would be *rude*."

His laughter, spontaneous and genuine, brought a smile to her face. She'd begun to worry the warrior had no sense of humor. Or worse, that he'd simply forgotten how to laugh.

"Careful now, don't split those stitches. They're meant to last the week, and if they do I won't need to apply them again. Go on, take a seat if you're lonesome. I could use you for a prayer."

He swallowed a chuckle, as surprised as she at his sudden outburst. He hadn't laughed like that in ages. As he watched her meticulously cleanse the altar, humming softly under her breath, he admired the almost subconscious deliberation she lavished on each motion. Though he'd long since learned to respect the priestess' devotion to the Morrigan, he could also recognize her as a master of her craft. *So few exhibit such discipline,* he lamented to himself.

"Your name, warrior."

Her voice - and her request - jarred him. "You mean I've not told you? Never introduced myself?" He stammered.

She smiled, a slow, mysterious smile. "I never asked. I appreciate you're a quick learner in not belaboring me with information I don't want, but now I need it. So if you would be so kind, give me your name please."

How strange she is, he thought. "Diarmuid."

"Don't be offended that I wouldn't know it, either," she said, using her rightmost ring finger to trace runes in oil upon a buxom stone figure. "The Morrigan has many heroes, and you'd be surprised at how long I've been doing this. But, I will say your name rings a bell."

Though he neither said nor expressed anything, she smiled again - more genuinely than she'd been wont to do before.

"Yes, that piques your vanity. But we're not here to do an exchange of backstories. Not yet, that is. Diarmuid, please step toward the dais."

He did as he was told, noticing almost instantly the settled and radiant energies that surrounded her consecrated space. Suddenly he felt almost ashamed of himself as he recalled hasty prayers and offerings, less tangible communions with the goddess that he thought before held superior weight.

"Mmmm, no, don't think so harshly of yourself," Qimmirea mused aloud, as though reading his mind. "If you watched me wield a sword, though I'm perfectly capable of defending myself, you would understand that there are some things we each are simply better at than others. That does not mean," she said, very kindly and

very sincerely, "that your prayers and your offerings
are any less noticed or appreciated by our Lady. You
wouldn't be here otherwise."

Before he could respond, she suddenly disrobed, then
stepped up next to him. Rolling her eyes at the shock on
his face, she placed a vial of oil into his hands. "Spare me
your fake modesty."

"On the contrary," he offered, "I'm wondering if you
need me to do the same."

"No thank you. It's enough for you to just draw the runes
as I tell you to, with intention. Possibly you're the only
person in this entire valley with the intention to invoke
this blessing, and I mean to take advantage of it if I can."

Suddenly he remembered the gifts by the entrance. "I'm
assuming you've... already had volunteers?"

"Too many. None worked." She tossed a handful of bones
into a stone bowl, then read the runes aloud. "*Ingwaz,
wunjo...*"

She paused, noticing that he'd twitched at that, and
dragged the bowl closer. "Look, I'm not making this up,
that's just what they say."

"Is there such a thing as loaded runes?" He mused aloud
as he stroked a line of oil dexterously across her chest. He
noticed, inconsequentially, that her breasts had stretch
marks. "What's the third?"

"*Fehu.* Yes, they're very cheeky today." She stepped away
from him and knelt at the base of the stone idol.

Looking down, he realized he stood just outside a thin

inlay of mother of pearl that ran in a ring around the altar. His alignment, with the sun setting outside behind him, cast his shadow across her prostrate figure. She leaned over, throwing her head back and tossing her arms to the ceiling, and he could see the oil gleaming faintly from an inner light that seemed cast from nowhere. A sudden hush descended. Then the rush of blood from his head to elsewhere in his body set his ears ringing.

He blinked. It was nighttime. The glow before him came from the hearth, not the altar, and his shadow sulked below him instead of shading over the naked priestess. Qimmirea, robed again, set a clay jug beside him and stretched.

"Sorry! You blacked out. That was... absolutely enough intention for a blessing," she shuddered, in a way that made Diarmuid blush.

"Don't look at me like that, drink up," she said, taking a swig from the jug before offering it up to him. The smell hit him just as the taste did, and he sighed in relief as strong spirits - the gods' greatest cordial - burned in his throat.

"*Ingwaz, wunjo, fehu.* I'm beginning to see why the goddess brought me here," he mumbled to himself.

"Yes. Do you think your time is up, warrior? That the goddess should call you, for you've accomplished your greatest feats?"

He didn't respond. He honestly couldn't.

"I'm not sure if that's absolute vanity or absolute slothfulness, but from looking at you," and she did, deeply, and intimately, as she took another draught from the jug, "I'm thinking it's simply crippling humility."

"Stop that," he warned. "I..."

"Don't know how to speak to someone about the truths
of yourself?" She interrupted calmly. "Don't know how
to put those truths to words, as much as you struggle to
put them to action? Why browbeat yourself so, Diarmuid.
You are a legend - and to be a legend before one's call to
the Morrigan, to have the world recognize one's merits
even as they still draw breath, is an envious trait indeed."

He squeezed his eyes shut, and tensed. Trust wasn't
an issue. Qimmirea, though he'd known her so briefly,
seemed to step immediately into a fiercely guarded haven
within the warrior's breast. Not simply from the fact she
had saved his life, and preserved his rank; but her own
candid nature, and her blunt honesty, gave her a right
few others in his life had achieved to understand and
recognize him as he was. There were simply walls that
had never come down. Walls even he couldn't breach.

"Why are you a priestess?" He asked suddenly. "What
put you on this path?"

She smiled, and swilled the contents of the jug
thoughtfully. "You actually want to know. That's
refreshing. Usually people just want to feel sorry for me."

"You're the most accomplished and devout follower of
the Morrigan I've ever met, and I *am* including myself,"
he pressed.

"No no, you don't have to flatter me. I'll tell you. I was
sold. Sold to the previous keeper of this oratory. You
know, that's what happens when you can't get rid of a
daughter the normal way."

He balked. "The normal way? You mean, married off?"

"You're surprised! How kind of you. I already told you, you don't have to flatter me. Yes, my parents had a devil of a time trying to find someone to wed me. It turns out that when all one brings to market are flaws, and criticisms, and resignation toward your daughter's failings, there aren't many buyers willing to take the risk and marry her despite them."

Her upright figure and stern jaw belied the pain evinced by those words. Diarmuid found himself surprised by her fortitude yet again. Brought up under such circumstances - told she had no worth, other than the worth others valued her at - and yet she still managed to act with such grace, and live with such confidence.

"Surely some would read between the lines of such unfavorable reports?" He offered awkwardly. Flirting was not his strongest suit.

Her brow darkened. "None rich enough, anyway. If they married me off to a poor man, they'd never be rid of me; what with too many children and the money from the farm finding its way into the bottoms of too many mugs of mead, etc. etc. No, far better investment to just sell me off to a druid, because then eventually I'd be able to pay for myself. And there's prestige in having a child who can speak to the gods. Certainly more prestige than having one in an unfavorable marriage. It's not unlike your own apprenticeship, though if I'm right and you are who I think you are, you didn't seem to let your unwished-for destiny in blacksmithing prevent you from becoming a warrior instead."

The jug made a humming noise as she drew her finger

along its lip. He looked at it meaningfully, and she laughed and passed it over. "I'll let you tell your own story when mine is finished. I make a much better listener than a storyteller, I promise. I too sought the Morrigan - thinking I'd served my purpose, done my time, and no longer had value among the living. She proved to me it was very much the reverse. My predecessor was old, too old to be bringing healthy young witches back from the brink of untimely deaths, and in saving my life she sacrificed her own. It took me a very, very long time to be thankful for that," she finished ruefully, casting the warrior a strange look. "So I can assure you, I understand the grudge you hold against me."

He grabbed her hand. Flirting bedamned. "If you'd died saving me, I'd be much more upset. But since neither of us were graced by the gift of the goddess, my ire is turned... elsewhere."

Never a flaw in his blade. Never a dent in his armor. The grace of the goddess to whom he sacrificed everything, bestowed upon everyone who crossed his path. Everyone but him.

It is not your time yet, warrior. I have yet to call for you, and until I call, you do not come.

II

FUNERAL RITES

Firelight flickers on her face, on the bright strands of her thick braids. He had never seen the priestess look so fierce, and regarded her with awe as she faced the massive trench carved up the side of the hill.

Behind him flowed the river Fyroe. Along the river's bank mingled the small population of Eillear, the village in which Diarmuid had found himself. Though funereal, the air seemed to vibrate with a latent sense of excitement. The Morrigan had called one of their own. And while death always brought grief, to they who loved the Lady of Death, it brought blessings as well.

A longboat of hewn wood soon came into view, slowly being poled up the river. A hush descended as the smoky light of torches lit the face of the corpse aboard. Gewinna, a respected elder; the ravages of time clear on her otherwise handsome features, with her streaming silver hair meticulously combed by her loving daughters and woven with ornaments of bone and flower.

The warrior had known Gewinna but little in his time among the Eillear. He knew she lived unmarried and that she had in her household only women, daughters she'd raised from orphans left behind by the Morrigan's call. She belonged to the old ways, this honored and respected shield maiden, had stood beside kings in battle on the bloody plains of Eire and faced the might of giants who had long since slunk away into the barren hills. When

she finally laid her shield to rest, she did so in the quiet
and fertile valley of Eillear, and the village that grew
up around her owed its bounty and its safety to the
protection of her name.

None were daring enough to face Gewinna in open
combat.

But as she grew older, and the gentle farmers and hearty
shepherds easy in the shadow of their protectress, raiders
and marauders grew more bold, daring to bite at the rosy
apple of Fyroe's ambling banks. It was from the worst of
these that Diarmuid had saved the beleaguered village.
And news of the slaughter, the lone warrior who slew a
host tenfold strong, carried far and wide.

Eyes followed him as he walked among them, and
whispers carried. The good woman, as well as her good
name, had died. Now they feared, and hoped, that his
spear would prove as effective as her shield in protecting
them all.

As the dirge slides onto the gravelly banks, men, their
heads uncovered, slowly drag it up the bank to the
trench over which Qimmirea stands. She begins to chant
in a low, but clear tone that carries from the pits of her
stomach and vibrates in her throat to fill the ears and
hearts of the villagers.

Diarmuid steps forward and takes up a place among the
men, shouldering the weight of the wooden dirge and
marching in step with them as they slide it into place. The
soft earth gives way to shovels, and Qimmirea's song is
carried in the throats of every unmarried woman present.
The rest stand guard, heads bowed, hands crossed. The
bridge between the living and the dead, a ritual built from
a mortal desire to pantomime ethereal and immaterial

ideals. Gewinna's body, already cold, lays in state in her funeral dirge as it slowly fills with the soil tossed by her neighbors and her family. At her feet lies a chest bearing the weapons she once wielded, and in her hands a shield. For the proud woman waged war in her youth, and many were the battles from which she emerged victorious.

As he watched, he could see the way she looked in combat, her golden hair bound in braids and her face twisted in ferocity with the blessings of the gods on her brow. The old kings and queens of Eire owed much to these warriors who fought for the sake of the glory of battle. Who warred amongst one another in passion and yet harmony, maintaining order among the chaos of the ancient and unruly civilizations. From their spear tips flowed blood, but from their tales of valor there came the beauty of dying so others may live in peace and bountiful plenty.

Do you remember the way the war horns sounded? He wonders, as he looks upon her peaceful face. *The pounding drums that matched the march of tireless feet? Do you resent your goddess for leaving you to live victorious on the battlefield? Do you thank her for letting you die instead in innocent silence, old and worn upon a bed of straw?*

Diarmuid noted other mounds carved in the riverbank and wondered the fate of those who slumbered there. Were they heroes? Kings, great masters of war and of might, who slew evil beasts for the honor of gods and men? What stories lay there beneath the earth that life no longer told?

Many burial sites like it exist in this long gone culture. Soft piles of earth that rise above the banks of rivers or along the ocean's shores. The warriors and the devout, the high chieftains and matriarchs, who rest after life's fitful

journey. Waiting for the final horns to sound, to call them
to the afterlife that promises so much more than the cold
ignominy of death. They tell their children stories, much
as their ancestors did before them, of the old gods who
wove the fate of humans, and who brought us the gifts of
life, and war, and beauty, and knowledge, and faith, and
death.

He looked up at the the priestess as she stood atop the
fresh mound. She wore a heavily embroidered robe sewn
with glittering threads of real gold, and on her ruddy
head she wore a circlet of hammered brass woven with
tiny crocuses. Stacked up her arms were bracelets of fine
metals, and on her fingers a smattering of rings, including
a tiny gold claddagh. She looked more impressive than
Diarmuid had ever expected she could, and he watched
with greater reverence as they buried Gewinna. The
Morrigan must have rated this woman most highly, that
her priestess would show such marked respect.

A raven circles overhead in the growing darkness.
Qimmirea's voice carries above even the sound of
shovelfuls of soil striking wood.

"Death calls for all of us. She watches from the bedside
of our birthing mothers, and she takes our hand as we
sink from this world into that of the next. There is only so
much she can tell us, only so much we can do to prepare
for her visit. But this much she makes clear - we must do
more than live only to die."

A cold wind rifles the dead grass, makes the bare trees
sigh and creak mournfully as she speaks. But huddled in
thick woolen cloaks and waiting for the blessing of their
goddess from the mouth of their devoted priestess, the
villagers stir not in discomfort or chill.

"Gewinna, beloved mother, respected lady," the priestess continues, "you leave behind a greater legend than you take away. Your soul has been called by the Lady, the Morrigan, but you do not die eternal so long as we who knew you can remember what you've done."

She bows her head. A small knot of singing girls, their voices quavering with emotion, dissolve into wailing tears. The centermost, a regal blonde named Aisla, takes from her head a circlet woven of flowers. She tosses the circlet upon the folded hands of her mistress, and throws her own to the heavens. Her eyes are dry, but they shine instead with a grief too deep for tears, too sharp for wailing agony.

"Ye've heard o' Rodval's Keep?" spoke a lad beside him, the shadow of age but a dusting of copper hair on his cheeks.

"Fenian an Crach," he added with a nod to the quiet warrior. A brief look of recognition flashed in Diarmuid's eyes.

"Rodval and his clan are dead, I thought," Diarmuid replied in a gruff voice, one not meant to be repellant yet unused to idle conversation.

"All but one," Fenian sighed, with a long look at the golden-haired girl who stood by the mound. "Gewinna were too late for the others. She laid justice swift, though."

There were no weapons left to tell tales of the faint scars on her flesh, and no survivors of the raiders that desecrated her home. Diarmuid breathes a sigh of relief. He knew the blade that spilled the blood of great Rodval. He is shocked to see the slim figure, standing in defiance of the death of her kindred.

The Morrigan did not call her, Diarmuid thought to himself as he watched the girl, now grown to a woman, pray wildly to the skies. *She is left to take a hero's place, to fill the void left behind as Gewinna is called to the beyond.*

He winces as Qimmirea's eye, fixed on Aisla, instead catches his own. The priestess could easily read the train of thoughts that crossed his brow. And just as easily can he read the not-so-subtle "I told you so" that crosses her own.

She thinks I am the hero who must raise that mantle. They all do, he realizes, as eyes from the crowd pass over him. *What matters it where I lay my spear? This land would do as well as any. There is no returning from where I have come.*

The moment passes. The earth above Gewinna settles, her burial mound rises complete. Her body awaits the final calling, the end of days when, alongside the other heroes buried along the riverbank, she can sail to meet the gods and join in feast and the glory of Tir na nOg.

As the crowds begin to disperse, he grabs a smoking stick of incense and slowly approaches the priestess. The strength of her ritual still makes itself felt in the energies surrounding her, but he can tell by the way she holds her shoulders, and the tremor in her lips, how exhausted she really is. He manages to reach her side and even place a hand upon her elbow before she notices him. But she smiles, and exhales, and he feels a tension dissipate almost instantly from her rigid form.

"Gewinna's loss will be felt for a long time," she said, and the shine of torchlight in her indigo eyes brightened as tears begin to fill them. "She stood for much that made our people great."

"She made sure to leave behind many who could take up the mantle, though," replied Diarmuid, as he watched several girls raise their own arms at Aisla's side, whispering prayers to augment their sister's.

"Yes. Aisla has already begun to fill our dear departed's shoes. But when you've watched at graves as long as I have," and she sighed as she spoke, the lines at the corners of her eyes and appearing upon her brow thrown into relief by the firelight, "you learn that those who come after are never like those who went before."

"You don't say whether or not you think them better or worse?" He pressed, looking sideways at her.

"It is not my job to judge the living. It is only my job to bury the dead."

She turned and swept away from the grave, her bare feet padding softly on the grassy path. He waited for a moment before following, and the tightly shut door of her quarters upon his arrival to the oratory told him he'd made the right call in giving her space.

He does not think of what it means, to leave those who knew him behind once he hears her fateful call. He does not know who would mourn him. But after watching that hero's burial, he realized that perhaps he has some work to do, some ties to bind him, before he can make that final journey.

O, Lady, who has guided my strength and my spear for so long, he prayed, out under the blanket of stars that glowed brightly above the oratory's kitchen garden. "I do not know whether I have outlived any sense of purpose, or simply have not truly begun to live at all. Has it all come and gone? Or am I yet to start?"

No answer met his plea. A single star fell through the heavens, its shining arc glowing with fury before sputtering out on the horizon. He watched it as it fell, embracing the silence of the dreaming wood and smelling the savory and sharp aromas of the few plants that struggled and bore against the frosts that still nipped in this late winter. Very few ornamental blossoms decorated the sparse plot. Though he was not well versed in the lore of flora and fauna used by wise women to cure and heal, he knew enough to recognize almost all that lay in the *bean feasa*'s well-tended garden. The only plants that seemed to grow for no purpose at all were a small patch of lilies, their green spears barely beginning to push from bulbs beneath the earth. Surrounding the lilies was a bed of shells and polished stones, meticulously placed in a radiating pattern that pleased Diarmuid with its symmetry and grace.

He knelt down, plucking free from the spaces between the border a few stubborn weeds. Then he laughed at himself.

"I, the great warrior Diarmuid, who once served in the forge of the legendary Jorgeir, smith of kings; I have found my calling in… weeding a witch's garden. Perhaps my Lady has a sense of humor after all."

Perhaps she has not abandoned me. I will not be a slave to ego, demand that which I have not earned. As he turned to regard the long houses of the village that glowed faintly with moonlight, he smiled. *I will find a purpose. My time is not yet done, and I have not yet served with all of me.*

It is unexpected, his first experience with death. When we

are young, all death comes as a surprise, no matter the hints she drops or the warnings that go unheeded. Youth has naught to do with death.

But they buried his mother, his kind and loving mother, from whose lips never a cruel word was said and whose hands had never once dealt him a harsh blow. They buried her by the sea, among grassy sand hills, over which bloomed the little white starflowers in the late spring.

She died early. The rest of the village fell not long after to fire and war, the everlasting constant that united the kingdoms of all Eire. He knew not the fate of his family, his neighbors, his friends. The forge in which he spent his childhood lay far from where he was born, and never again did he see any who would tie him to that early place. Then his ears filled with the calling of the Morrigan and to none other, from that point, would he listen. For no other purpose did he swing his arm.

What a waste, he could hear in the voice of the priestess. He snorted. She seemed to challenge him, an experience to which he was unused.

Would he rise to it?

—

Miri woke late the next morning, a luxury to which she was unaccustomed. She tread softly into the kitchen, where a merry fire burned in the hearth and water boiled on the oven hob.

"The goddess preserve me. What's all this, then?" She asked, eyes wide in wonder. She stepped out into the garden, noticing instantly the patch of weeds cleared from the flowerbed and a sizeable stack of firewood placed neatly in the grate beside the door.

"Hmm. I suppose this means he thinks he's staying," she mumbled to herself, turning back into the oratory and lighting incense upon the altar. She knelt before her stone idol, peering shrewdly at the goddess' impassive face.

"I know not what you're about, my Lady. But I have ever served you without question, and I'm not about to stop now. Just... be gentle," she pleaded, putting a worn hand over her breast.

"Please."

III

A ONCE GREAT KING

There lurked danger in the eyes of the king. As Diarmuid approached, he knelt in deference. King Hrothgir, a mighty force, had earned the throne upon which he sat, bathed in blood of his enemies and borne with the strength of his arms. Even now, as the lines on his swarthy face deepened and the bones that upheld such a mighty frame creaked in winter months, Diarmuid knew he'd be hard pressed to hold his own against such a foe.

But Hrothgir's eyes, though dangerous, were warm. And his face, though lined, broke into a welcoming smile as the warrior approached.

"They call you Diarmuid, the savior of Eillear," his voice was deep, and in its depths there lay the mystical tones of the ancient tongue.

"They do," replied the warrior, knees and head still bent.

"I see this title does not rest easily on your strong shoulders. Stand, Diarmuid."

He did. Long did the king study the warrior's pensive face, and nothing escaped his searching gaze.

"Hmm. Then perhaps it's time you performed a feat worthy of such a claim, is that what you're thinking? You answer the king's call for the mightiest warrior in Eire. So perhaps some of you believes this claim after all, though the rest of you may deny it to yourself."

Diarmuid bristled, but the king chuckled, waving his hand in pardon. "What matters it. I have need of a warrior, and here a warrior has come. Brynhilde!"

From behind a misty curtain a woman appeared. Tall, dark, though not so much as her father, with eyes of sapphire - blue as Diarmuid's own - and twisted locks of golden hair that reached her feet. Though her ornaments were few all were wrought of the finest silver, and her robes dyed a deep and brilliant indigo.

"My daughter. Lovely, no?" Hrothgir gruffed at Diarmuid.

"Fair met, maiden," replied Diarmuid, with a nod toward the stately lass. He turned toward Hrothgir, eyebrow raised. "If this calling be for what I think it is, I'm afraid I must remind my good king that I am bound by oath to remain unwed. I serve the calling of the Morrigan, and she will be supplanted by no other maiden… no matter how fair."

The king threw back his head and laughed, long and heartily. Brynhilde covered her mouth with a long, fluttering sleeve, but Diarmuid saw her eyes were dancing.

"'*Oath*', he says. Were it not for your oath, I'd tell ye to get in line. It is not for lack of suitors I called you here on behalf of my Brynhilde, but an abundance of them!"

Brynhilde swallowed a chuckle of her own, turning her limpid gaze on Diarmuid. "It is your might, great warrior, that my father is in need of. My hand is promised to a king whose wondrous deeds and mighty kingdom even you may have heard tell of. But his claim is not," she sighed, "so easily laid in this land. You see, he cannot leave his country unprotected to seek me out, and the blood of my fathers," she said proudly, "cannot be won without combat. My betrothed must battle and best three other claimants before he can rightfully wed me and grant his name to my children."

"I am but one champion," Diarmuid replied in confusion. "You wish me to seek this mighty king and offer myself as foe, so he may win you?"

"No, Diarmuid. That arrangement, I am sure, would suit neither of you," she answered, eyes dancing in merriment again. "My suitor seeks a proxy, a champion who can fight on his behalf three foes of this country. Should you succeed, he is willing to offer my dowry as his reward."

Diarmuid put up his hands in denial, once again bowing deeply. "I accept no gold or lands for my deeds of might. The honor of victory, and your own goodly graces, will be reward enough."

King Hrothgir studied him for a moment. "Where is it you hail from, champion?"

"I would... rather not say," replied Diarmuid quietly.

"Surely you've a home to return to once you leave from here," he insisted. "The home of your birth matters not. But who in Eillear offers shelter to their revered hero?"

The warrior smiled faintly. He could only imagine the look on Qimmirea's face were a king's bounty brought to her doorstep.

"You've heard of the wise woman that lives outside the

village? The priestess Qimmirea?"

Again the rafters rang with the laughter of the massive king.

"Good soul Miri! Aye, you'll receive your reward yet, champion, whether ye take it or no." He continued to chuckle, and Diarmuid noticed a faraway expression, accompanied by the faintest blush, that crossed the king's face. Brynhilde rolled her eyes with an exasperated smile at her father, then turned back to Diarmuid.

"I see the battle appeals more to you than the bounty. I suppose I could take that as an affront to my charms," she said lightly, with a somewhat stern look, "but I owe you my reputation, so I will only say, you have my faith. And on behalf of my betrothed, I accept you as his proxy to do battle against the foes who would supplant him and win my hand in his stead."

She drew an ornate dagger from its sheath in her breast, tapping it lightly upon Diarmuid's bowed shoulder. "You will meet the first of them tomorrow. You are welcome to the bounties of the hall until each battle is wrought."

The great hall rang with feasting, for the mood was light and all knew of the competition that would begin on the morrow. Heaped over the table were trenchers of stew, haunches of meat, and platters of roast potatoes that all sent forth their heady aroma to mingle with the incense and smoke from the hall's great fires. Men and women from all of Bjirtka joined the clamor, feasting at the board of their great king and sharing tales of his magnificent deeds of might and strength. Like many of their tribe they eagerly anticipated the feats of martial prowess that were promised. Though they looked upon the champion as an outsider they respected the name he earned for himself among the people of Eillear. Many times did he find his horn full of mead, and many voices rang to the honor of the beautiful Brynhilde and the mighty arm of the champion who would win her a king for a mate.

The day dawned bright and clear. A ring, formed around an open space before the stone stronghold, marked the place in which the two combatants meant to do battle. Diarmuid, armed only with spear and leather armor that allowed him to move freely and quickly, stepped into the ring. A hush descended as he waited to meet his opponent.

Suddenly the crowd parted. Up walked a mountain of a man with wild black eyes and curled black hair. He bore a massive axe, that stood almost as long as Diarmuid was tall, and he wore a coat of maille and a helm of hammered iron. Upon seeing his opponent, the man spat, and roared in fury.

"Is this all the milksop King Ulle thinks to send in his stead? No wonder he leaves not the halls of his dainty palace. Why, I could snap you asunder with naught but a breath!" boasted the challenger.

"I am Diarmuid, the champion of Brynhilde. Do you challenge this king in his suit of the princess?" replied Diarmuid calmly, ignoring the jibes of his opponent.

"The lad speaks so softly, he hath the heart and the voice of a woman," scoffed the man. "Aye, I, Dag Boor, challenge the weakling Ulle, and will win me the hand of Brynhilde in his stead."

"Then draw your weapon and fight. This is a battle of steel, and not of words," returned Diarmuid, leaning easily on the butt of his spear.

Dag Boor spat again, and with a wild roar swung his axe overhand at Diarmuid's reclining form. A split second before the blade could hew him asunder, Diarmuid pivoted in place, swinging nimbly out of the axe's wide arc.

A screech of metal grated on the ears of the audience. Dag Boor, foreseeing Diarmuid's dodge, had deftly twisted the axe in its swing to turn it wide; and Diarmuid, keen to the warrior's expert control over his heavy weapon, had stuck the spear behind him to intercept the blow.

Grunting in anger, Dag Boor stepped back, then threw himself forward again in another overhanded attack. Diarmuid, knowing the giant relied on the strength of his maille to turn the point of his spear away, did not strike at the obvious opening. Instead he pivoted again, dancing around him as lightly as if he were on a walk in an open field.

"Will you only dance then, you lightskirt? Will not you fight?" Spittle formed in the corners of the brutish warrior's mouth as he raged, taking swipe after swipe at the dexterous champion.

Again Diarmuid ignored his jibes. The words of fools lay lightly on his brow. And in battle, there was only one call he listened for. He strained mightily to hear her, with every turned blow and every dodged attack he listened, in vain, for the voice of the Morrigan.

He heard nothing. As much as he focused on her ethereal command, only going through the motions of battle with Dag Boor, he couldn't help but notice the opening that gaped below his opponent's arm in the maille, a loose point the warrior clearly believed he protected with the sheer bulk of his muscles.

Finally Diarmuid grew tired of the game, frustrated with the effort of listening for a call that would never come. Once more, the giant swung his axe overhead for a strike he was sure would split the champion in half.

Today is not my day to die, it seems.

Until it fell from nerveless fingers into the dust now muddy with his own blood.

Today, it is his.

Diarmuid, waiting for the perfect opportunity, had thrust his spear directly into the gap in Dag Boor's maille. It passed through the man's shoulder, and then his collarbone, slicing his neck and the bottom of his jaw before being wrenched free by Diarmuid's powerful strike. The crowd gasped in shock at the sudden end to the fierce battle, and then began to cheer.

"I have bested the first opponent, Dag Boor," Diarmuid said, kneeling in the dust before Brynhilde. "His axe is yours, to bring to your betrothed as proof of his might."

"That you have, my champion. And two remain, that is," she said, the blood draining from her face as she cast a look at the crumpled corpse of the defeated challenger bleeding out in the center of the ring, "if they don't withdraw their challenges after such a display of might."

Diarmuid simply nodded, then rose at Brynhilde's behest. He vanished into the great hall to clean his spear, leaving behind the milling crowd that had begun to clear Dag Boor's body from the ring.

Two more challengers. The next was a whey-faced warrior from the fens who fought with cunning, but could not best the spear that seemed to move like lightning through the air. He too, collapsed in the center of the ring, choking on blood that gurgled from a hole torn in his throat.

The third posed a very different sort of challenge. They brought to bear a shield, and they too wore a helm of hammered iron. But even before they removed it, Diarmuid straightened in shock.

"But, you are a maiden," he spoke, as the warrior entered the ring. "What claim have you to the hand of Brynhilde?"

"It is not my sister's hand I seek to win, champion." The woman removed her visor. Those who could see her features gasped in recognition, for they mirrored Brynhilde's own.

"Valka!" shrieked Brynhilde, rushing into the ring in fury. "What are you doing here?"

"Making my claim as the bride of King Ullc, a claim you so viciously stole from me," she spat in return. Brynhilde stumbled backwards, her bronze cheeks turning pale with shock.

"Valka! What is the meaning of this?" roared King Hrothgir, his dark face lowering in rage. "You were banished from Bjirtka, and rightfully so, for calling upon dark and forbidden magic."

"What say you then, sister?" Brynhilde seethed. "What treachery can you accuse me of, when compared to yours?"

"None that you would own, you viper. But my reckoning lies not with you. It lays with your champion, who stands and watches us with cunning and wonder. Champion!" She spoke fiercely, her piercing blue eyes riveted on Diarmuid's own. "Do you accept my challenge?"

The warrior sighed, and turned to Hrothgir. "Will this count? Does her claim meet the challenge of defeating three suitors on behalf of Brynhilde's betrothed?"

King Hrothgir cast a look of unfathomable sadness upon the woman, one Diarmuid didn't expect him capable of. "Daughter," he spoke softly, and though he did not rise from his throne, his voice carried. "Do you pursue this challenge, a fight to the death?"

"Yes, King Hrothgir, I do," she returned, the strength and vicious anger still bright in her fearless eyes. "I am not your daughter, and she is not my sister. Neither of you deserve the title. And since I have been exiled from the hall of Bjirtka I no longer carry your name or your blood. Champion! Accept my challenge!" She cried, throwing down her shield at Diarmuid's feet.

She wields her sword like a fury. The Morrigan herself fuels the wrath of this one's hand. I wonder what it is that drives her so; and I wonder which of us the Morrigan will call this day.

"I accept."

"Then fight!"

She dropped into a crouch, slipping her shield back onto her arm in one swift movement. Diarmuid angled his spear toward one of the leather straps, but did not move quickly enough to cut it free from her arm. She snapped her arm back with violent force, nearly ripping the spear from Diarmuid's iron grip.

If he moves like lightning, she moves like wind. Everywhere he strikes, a resounding knock of metal on wood rings through the clearing, her shield withstanding every thrust. He knows her arm will grow tired eventually but she too presses him hard with swipes of her short sword into every available opening.

"Do you truly seek the Morrigan then, Valka?" He asked her, after a flurry of blows rendered them both momentarily winded.

"I seek my truth, warrior. I seek my end, whether that end be found today or a hundred years from now."

She speaks with deadly conviction. But he sees the ravens beginning to circle, drawn by the smell of blood and the heat of battle. His goddess watches them both. He knows not which of them would fall.

For a moment he hesitates. He fears what she said; to live today, and die in a hundred years. Diarmuid had no desire to survive for a hundred years, to live like this, chasing the call of the Morrigan. He could fall to a blow of that mighty sword. He could die in the heat of battle, his body raised on the shields of those who knew his strength, and his soul could fly from its mortal bondage to the side of his beloved goddess.

But he sees beyond the anger in Valka's fierce blue eyes. He sees their poignant desperation, the end of their hope, the depths of despair that knows her fate is sealed and her future signed by hands other than her own. And he knows that despite listening for it with every fiber of his being, this day, the call of the Morrigan falls on her ears instead of his.

"You cannot win against fate, shield maiden," he responded sadly. "Just as I cannot defy my own to save you. I am sorry."

She raises her shield one last time. She thrusts her sword at Diarmuid's throat. She releases a feral cry, one that pierces the heavens, one that, if he listens closely, faintly echoes of "Brynhilde!"

His spear slides past the shield and into Valka's heart.

"Go to her, maiden," whispered Diarmuid, as the dying woman's head drooped on his shoulder. "No matter your fate, the Morrigan calls to you."

Valka spat. And then, with a gasp, she died.

"Thank you."

Diarmuid did not lower her body to the ground. Instead he lifted it, carrying Valka to where her sister stood, watching in horror with her hands covering her face. He laid the slain maiden at her sister's feet, and he kneeled.

"Your third opponent is defeated, princess. As the champion chosen on behalf of your betrothed, I have vanquished his foes and won him your fair hand."

Brynhilde, her eyes riveted to the lifeless body of her sister, said nothing. King Hrothgir stood and put a hand on her shoulder, turning toward Diarmuid.

"You have won for King Ulle the honor of my blood. But we... will not feast this day. For three days," he said, turning to the gathered crowd, "we will mourn the slain

Valka, who once was the daughter of your king."

The crowd murmured amongst themselves, watching as the king bent and lifted Valka's body into his own arms. He walked slowly into the long hall, followed by Brynhilde, who was supported by Diarmuid.

The gates shut and the crowds slowly dispersed.

"We were twins," Brynhilde began sadly, the brightness of tears dimming the brilliance of her eyes. She and Diarmuid sat in the darkened hall, the dying embers of the hearth fire their only light. King Hrothgir had taken Valka's body to his own couch, there to watch and see that no evil spirits stole her soul or desecrated her body as they mourned her. "As babes, an ancient crone, a *bean feasa* like your Miri, came to our mother and offered a blessing upon her children. My mother accepted, delighted that the gods would so recognize the fruit of her womb. But she didn't realize that ancient crone was a woman my mother had thwarted ages ago, and one who had since sworn unholy vengeance upon her and her family. She turned to our cradle, and she stroked both our foreheads, and she began to chant as though a vision had come upon her.

'One child will grow, unparalleled in beauty and in grace. One child's hand will be won by the might of a great king. One will live long, beloved by this land, and will leave it with the honor of her fathers to bring forth a great line of mighty kings in a land far from here. One child, this blessing falls upon,'

"And then she turned, and stared into my mother's eyes, and laughed a hideous laugh, 'and never shall ye know which child it is that bears this blessing! Not til the other shall fall dead, weeping blood, at the feet of her hated sister!'"

Brynhilde sniffed, covering her mouth with her hands. "My mother was paralyzed. She couldn't hide the old hag's visit, or lie about what she'd said. There were many witnesses, and all heard every word of the dread woman's curse. We both grew up together, knowing one day one of us would die alone and unloved, and the other live a perfect life. We promised each other," she sobbed into her hands, "we promised we would love each other no matter what. We even tried to swear vows when our mother died. Vows that we would never wed, but instead live with and for one another, so neither of us could suffer the curse."

"Then, what happened? How came your sister to be banished?" prompted Diarmuid, before Brynhilde was lost to her tears.

"It... it was Ulle. Before he was a king, he came to our kingdom as a ransomed son. Our own brother, Darothil, was sent to his father's court in exchange. A common practice, to bring up one son in the family of the other, so the two kingdoms would know peace and not war with one another. And as much as my sister and I loved each other," Brynhilde sighed, "we both loved Ulle. My sister, she always had stronger passions, and in my eyes, greater beauty than I. I had almost resigned myself to my fate, that Ulle would see her and love her, and that I was to be the cursed child, the hated sister. But Valka, she didn't want to wait to find out which of us Ulle would pick. She sought out the wise woman, and demanded to know which of us the hag had cursed."

"Did she find her?"

"No. It is believed the *bean feasa* is dead. Or even that she

was a goddess herself in disguise, sent down to wreak
vengeance on my mother for the wrong she did. Instead
Valka... she performed a ritual, an act of dark magic,
hoping she could see through the veil and learn the truth
of the witch's curse. When my father learned of it, he was
furious, and he banished Valka from our lands. He said
she could have brought down the wrath of the gods upon
our people, and to do so in an act of such selfishness was
that for which no daughter of his would ever be forgiven.
So she left," finished Brynhilde mournfully, dissolving
into tears. "And now my dear sister is dead, and it's all
my fault."

The warrior knew not how to comfort the grieving
maiden. He awkwardly put out a hand to stroke her
head, bent over as it was while she sobbed. Slowly she
subsided, swallowing mightily and trying to smile
bravely.

"You have done well, champion. You have defeated all
three claimants, and I am now free to live with my Ulle,
and bear his children, who will be mighty kings. I owe
you much, and I thank you for the swift and gracious
death you bestowed upon my sister. She died in battle,
and so now the Morrigan will claim her soul, and
hopefully offer her in the afterlife what she never could
have in this one."

The Morrigan called her, thought Diarmuid, as he
remembered the circling ravens that wheeled above in the
clear blue sky. *She will find glory in the afterlife, though she
so mistakenly wasted her time here.*

"I thank you for your tale, princess," he stood and bowed,
lightly kissing the tips of her fingers. "And I honor your
betrothed for allowing me to wield my spear in battle
in his stead. May you live long, and happy, and let no

shadow of shame or guilt," he said, touching her chin with his fingertips and smiling with a grace that she felt in her soul, "be cast upon that happiness. You have done no wrong. Until the Morrigan calls for your soul, protect it and its innocence as well as you can."

She nodded with a shaky smile, and with a final bow, he turned and left the stronghold.

—

"Do you mind explaining to me," cried Miri dazedly several days later, "why a host of King Hrothgir's finest warriors just marched in state up through the high road of Eillear and laid a chest of gold and jewels at my doorstep?"

"Do you want the short story, or the long one?" He replied laconically from the kitchen hearth where he lounged, idly peeling potatoes.

"Hmm." She plunked the chest down on the heavy wooden table, then sat staring at both it and Diarmuid bemusedly.

"The long one, please."

IV

LOVESTRUCK,

BLOOD SUCK

"There's a messenger here for you."

Miri's tone as she said it made Diarmuid pause, and he stopped in the doorway to regard her for a moment. She looked extra thorny this morning. A thundercloud rested on her freckled brow and a pout puckered her small, but round pink lips as she vigorously dug weeds from her lily bed.

"If it's a messenger you didn't care to see, will he be one I'm likely to welcome?" Diarmuid asked diplomatically.

"*She*, will not give you the option. She's made herself at home in the altar place. If you would be so kind as to see what she wants so she will leave, I'd appreciate it. I've a ritual to attend to."

He doubted that. The discordant energies she was giving off made even him uncomfortable, and he knew she would never so disturb her goddess. Miri made it a point of pride that she never brought her mortal cares to the feet of the stone idol, and he often honored her for it. But not stopping to argue, he simply nodded in assent and stepped into the cool stone oratory.

Instantly he realized exactly what it was about the visitor that had so raised Miri's ire. She lifted imperious amber eyes, shaded by heavy brows of raven black. Her hair, of the same color, she wore held back from her high forehead with a circlet of the finest silver upon which emeralds and pearls were studded. Voluminous robes of colored silks draped from her slim and stately form, flowing over the impeccably clean stone floor of the altar. He noticed her hem crossed the thin mother-of-pearl inlay that circled the stone idol and understood the discordance in Miri's energies. Respect for any being that was not herself - god or mortal - clearly did not come naturally to this woman.

He shifted his glance to the entryway that led to the oratory's entrance and into the graveyard. On either side stood two sentries clad in maille and studded leather armor, with iron helms on their erect heads and spears clutched tightly in their plate-covered fists. He smothered a sigh and bowed to the stranger, though he recognized her not.

"Rise, Diarmuid," she said with a stately wave of her hand. "I've heard tell of you, and I know your presence does as much honor to me as mine does to you."

"An honor," he said apologetically, his head still bowed, "that I wish I knew more of. To whom do I owe this unexpected visit?"

"I am Queen Niamh, of Arbannen." He frowned, and then a look of recognition crossed his face. She smiled.

"Yes, I figured my kingdom was not completely unknown to you. Nor my druids, who, despite what the priestess who lives here may have you believe, walk in the grace and the blessing of the Morrigan."

Ah. So there was more to Miri's dislike than that of entitled royalty. He began plotting exactly how to pry the tale from the taciturn priestess.

"Regardless," she continued, clearing her throat, and he returned his full attention to her. "My request is for you, and I was told I could find you here. So I will... inconvenience... her as little as possible."

"A request for me, Your Grace?" He echoed, eyebrows raised.

"Yes. Your prowess in battle has spread far and wide. But I understood, too," she said, her eyes glittering, "that there is more than strength behind the spear you wield. My predicament requires both intelligence and might, and I'm hoping it is one I can entrust to you at your utmost discretion."

He waited, neither assenting nor dissenting. One must always carefully gauge the requests of royalty, and not pledge oneself to more than one should. She realized he knew this, and she smiled with slightly more sincerity.

"Fine, I will tell you first. My life," she said dramatically, "is in the greatest peril."

Again, he responded not. His eyes drifted to the sentries standing guard, both of whom were in clear earshot. She understood his gaze and frowned.

"Yes, it is a danger even my most faithful guards cannot seem to thwart." She beckoned for him to sit again, and this time he did. "During the last full moon, for three straight nights, I was... attacked, in my sleep. The night before, the night of, and the night after. Each night I woke in a different place. The first, in the palace gardens, the second, in the great hall, and the third," she shuddered in recollection, "upon the roof of the tallest tower. I nearly fell to my death, and would have if my lethargy upon my wakening had not kept me rooted in place. Every morning I woke, it was with the most peculiar drained sensation. My blood ran sluggish, my lips and throat parched, and I struggled all day with great weakness."

"Did you seek a healer?" He prodded, though from the description of her complaints he well knew the creature that may have caused them.

"I sought my own druids. On the third day they bathed me in ewe's milk and fed me a diet of only meat, and I woke the next day refreshed and reinvigorated. Whatever it is that attacked me, it has not come again since. But the full moon is nigh, and I fear this fiend's return. Do you know what it is that haunts me?" She pleaded. In her eyes, as insincere as they tended to be, he saw real and paralyzing fear.

He nodded. "It's a vampyr. An ancient fae; a succubus or incubus, the manifestation of unrequited love. Have you any... err... rejected or lovelorn suitors, milady?"

She scoffed, in a dismissive way that didn't sit well with Diarmuid. "I'm a queen, unwed, of one of the most powerful and wealthy kingdoms in Eire. I have many lovers, and many who would seek to share my throne. Must I parade each and every one out until they confess?"

He shrugged. "Most likely not. It is enough that it confirms my theory. I can rid you of this creature, your majesty, however," he hesitated, lacing his fingers together tightly, "I will need to wait in your... err, bedchamber, for each of the three nights in order to adequately track the fiend."

She didn't even blush, just nodded. He breathed a sigh in relief. For a moment neither spoke, and then suddenly Queen Niamh rose from her seat. Diarmuid too stood, and bowed again.

She smirked. "So formal. You would fit in well at my court. If I could only trade those ragged hides for silken attire..." She laughed at the disgusted expression he was unable to keep from his face, then without another word swept away, beckoning her guards to attend her.

"She thinks I hate her druids?" Miri's mischievous smile brought out a wrinkle on the bridge of her nose when Diarmuid told her the tale of the Queen's visit. "That whelp. They've got her wrapped around their slim white fingers and she'll never even know it. The druids of Arbannen can trace their lineage back to the fae folk. I'd never do them an ill turn. We each practice in our own way, and take care not to tread on one another's toes. I've joined them on a few seances," and she blushed faintly, "and I'm sure you'll see them partake of ours."

"Well, now I'm interested," he said earnestly, but she shook her head with a coy smile.

"You'll just have to wait for Beltane like everyone else - unless you visit Niamh's court. If you're into that sort of thing."

"Seances?"

"No," she rolled her eyes. "Royalty."

He shrugged. "King Hrothgir seems as down to earth as the rest of us, does he not?"

"King Hrothgir is the last king of the old ways. I see
that in his son. When men no longer have to strive for
greatness, they instead find value in other, more worldly
things. Queen Niamh has always sat upon a silken pillow
in her marble court. What knows she of strife, and war,
and famine? No, she surrounds herself with courtiers,
painted men and women who have never felt the heft of a
spear nor drawn the blood of another living being. They
play at games of wit, and cunning, and think because
their minds are broader than their forebears that they live
a life above them. But this isn't fair of me, actually," she
said, with a guilty look. "I shouldn't let my opinion color
yours. I just..." she bit her lip - a rather cute expression,
Diarmuid couldn't help but notice - "I feel akin to you
somehow; and it's been so long since I've had a kindred
spirit with which to air my grievances."

He smiled reassuringly. "Fear not. Your secrets are safe
with me. And I promise to give Queen Niamh and her
court a fair and honest judgement."

He frowned suddenly, hesitant to ask the witch's opinion
on the beast he faced. "What know you of the vampyr?"

Her face grew grave. "Is that what troubles her. I owe
the queen an apology. That is no minor threat; no
insignificant bad magic cast upon her court. A vampyr
means she has a powerful enemy, and that you," she said,
eyeing him meaningfully, "have your work cut out for
you."

"Who would want to harm the queen in this way? It
seems irrational. Murdering her wouldn't put them on
her throne."

"Hmm. You're right. Something doesn't quite track. But I

have seen the many, many forms thwarted love can take," she added, a slightly haunted look marring her usually cheerful expression, "and those who suffer from it make grave mistakes."

They were silent for a moment, each thinking of the nature of this beast and from whence it spawned.

Miri looked at him, her eyes unfathomable, her chin cradled in the palm of her hand. "You may have to find this creature's conjurer. A vampyr is no easy feat of summoning, and there's no telling what they may do when they discover you've defeated it."

"You think perhaps a sorcerer of some kind is at the bottom of this?"

"A sorcerer, or more likely someone wealthy enough to pay for one. And if they're wealthy enough to buy a sorcerer, they've the resources to wreak plenty of havoc."

"Niamh herself said she could have many enemies. She seems to have," he swallowed uncomfortably, "many lovers, none of whom she intends to wed. I can't possibly investigate all of them, not in the span of three days."

Miri paused for a moment to ponder again, scratching her strong chin thoughtfully with a rough finger. "The vampyr must return to its master and feast upon their blood. If you follow it, you may learn of the truth behind these attacks. I know not if the vampyr must drink from the sorcerer, or the invoker," she clarified apologetically, "but one should hopefully lead you to the other."

"You are wise, and your advice is sound," he agreed candidly. "I will follow the vampyr on the first night and wait for it to drink of its master's blood. Then the next day I can inquire of his identity and hopefully prevent the beast from feeding again."

A solid plan.

Until it didn't work.

First, though he was in fact welcome to watch and wait from the queen's bedchambers, the queen failed to actually appear in them herself. He began to worry that the vampyr had attacked her before she could reach it until suddenly a maid entered the room.

"Hail, maiden. Where lies your mistress?" He asked curtly, once she'd finished shrieking about murderers in her mistress' chambers and he'd finished reassuring her that he was absolutely supposed to be there.

"She... they was playing hunt the hare," the girl stammered, still shaken. "Milady told me to... she stays in a lord's chamber this night. I was to bring her night things."

Diarmuid had to close his eyes to prevent himself from rolling them. "Take me to the chamber, if you would be so kind."

"Oh but, sir, I don't think she's open to another threeso-"

"Just take me there, please."

The girl gulped and nodded. He followed her down the spiraling tower, then along a corridor lined with stately oak doors. From many came squeals, and moans, and other sounds of licentious and raucous behavior that Diarmuid could only shake his head at.

"She... it's this one, my lord," the girl stammered, and she took out a large brass key and fitted it to the lock. Diarmuid, not trusting the state of dress - or frankly, the nature of the activities of its current occupants - chose not to enter behind her. He instead peered through the brief gap in the door, noticing an oriel above an open fireplace.

"Do you... should I leave you the key, my lord?" The girl asked nervously when she returned to the hallway.

Diarmuid had spotted an open balcony at the end of the corridor, only two doors down from the room in which the queen lay. "No. Take the key, and tell no one that the queen is not in her normal bedchamber this night."

"Y...yes sir."

Now I get to decide whether the vampyr will come to the queen's bedchamber, or this one. A nuisance.

He stepped out onto the balcony, peering past the glowing windows of the castle into the murky gloom beyond. All was still.

All but a mysterious black figure, that danced eerily across the moonlit sky.

"Got you," muttered Diarmuid to himself.

Stepping out onto the slim stone ramparts that led from the balcony to the windows beyond, he moved in the shadows, slowly approaching the batlike monster as it neared the bedchamber. He had to dodge the light that still spilled forth from some windows and avert his eyes from the occupants behind them, who apparently did not believe in the necessity of drawing the curtains despite the nature of their activities. Shifting to a wider stance, he balanced lightly on the balls of his feet, drawing back his spear as the vampyr fluttered closer.

It alighted on the iron railing, then shrieked as it spotted Diarmuid lying in wait in the shadows. Baring fangs glistening with blood, it swiped a fist at the warrior. Diarmuid dodged its strike, jabbing his spear at the monster's chest, but the awkward angle and the precarious nature of his balance caused him to miss.

The creature seemed to want to press its advantage. It whirled into the moonlit sky, then darted at Diarmuid, clawed feet extended and gripping for his shoulder. Diarmuid allowed the creature to close with him, hoping he could bear it down from the sky and pin it to the ramparts in one dexterous maneuver.

He did not account for the creature's speed.

It lifted him from the ledge, and for a moment Diarmuid hung, suspended in midair by its grip. The vampyr dithered briefly, unsure whether to simply release the warrior to fall to his death or try to bring him elsewhere to feast. Diarmuid's blood ran hot, and the beast was hungry.

Its indecision cost it its foot.

Whipping a knife from his boot Diarmuid sliced with all his strength through the vampyr's tendon, severing it to the ankle and turning the raking talons to nerveless, limp appendages. As he dropped from the beast's grasp, he reached out for the iron railing, flexing his forearms hard and grunting as his entire weight slammed onto the side of the castle, hanging from his tenuous grip.

While he managed to cling desperately to safety the

creature let out a feral screech, diving again at the glass window separating it from its prey. But instead of shattering the thin panes, it ricocheted off as though repelled by some unseen force. Diarmuid watched in some surprise, wondering what magics the queen would have access to strong enough to repel a vampyr, before he recalled the druids that were said to live within the castle.

Niamh's druids must've done more than restore her blood. If Miri knew the nature of the vampyr then I bet they did, too.

Shaking the train of thought from his mind, he focused instead on pulling himself back up to the ledge to challenge the vampyr once again. As it realized that more than just the warrior stood between it and its target, it circled among the stars angrily, yowling and spitting in bitter ire.

Diarmuid wondered what the people of the castle thought of its strange and wild noises, then realized with chagrin they weren't too far off from the noises they themselves were making.

"Royalty," he spat, commiserating completely with Miri's earlier rant.

It made a few more halfhearted attempts to dive at the window, but between the point of Diarmuid's spear and the protection spell cast by the druids, it had no chance of penetrating to the chamber within. Finally, it seemed to give up, spreading its wings and soaring up toward one of the further towers of the castle.

"Must be hungry," muttered Diarmuid to himself as he watched it spiral into the night sky. "Let's see if I can follow it and discover the master who controls it." And he did, making his way back to the open balcony and running nimbly down the long corridor.

He only got lost twice. At last, he stumbled upon the passage that led to the far tower - and directly into one of Niamh's fabled druids.

"Uh," he stammered, as the ethereal and unworldly beauty of the woman before him caused his mind to blank. She wore her ebony black, softly curling hair parted in the center of her crown and twisted into two long braids that she tucked into a fine silver belt. Her eyes were exquisite amethyst, and the brows that arched over them were fine, and high, and perfectly symmetrical. She smiled at him with her thin, but shapely, red lips.

"I see you seek the incubus too," she said, by way of greeting. "You must be the warrior Diarmuid."

"So it... did you uh. See anyone?" He stammered lamely, still dazed by her beauty.

"I saw it come this way, but I know not who it seeks. Only myself and my sister live within this tower," and she frowned slightly.

He began to realize that perhaps it was not only the queen who wielded love like a weapon in this strange and wonderful castle. The druid's dress, cut open to her navel, exposed her milk white chest and shapely breasts. He could smell the heat of sex emanating from her like a perfume. Despite her uncanny beauty it struck a discordant note in him - one that shook him from his daze, allowing him to suddenly and clearly see the truth.

"You and the queen have the same lover," he said flatly.

She actually looked surprised.

"You... well. That is quite... astute of you. And you think it is this lover who plagues the queen?"

Her eyes seemed to challenge him, daring him to name her as the conjurer of the incubus. But he smiled a disarming smile, one that she realized came from a heart and a soul more cunning than any hero of the Morrigan she'd ever faced before.

"No. What use have you for a throne? You already serve at the altar of a being that transcends petty kings and queens."

She looked sad, and at the mention of her goddess actually hung her head in shame. "I tried to stop him. He wanted me, and when he knew he couldn't keep me, he thought he could try to incite my jealousy and my wrath by instead seeking the love of the queen. I don't think it sat well with him," and she sighed, in a sort of patronizing way that Diarmuid didn't like, "to be rejected by two very powerful and very unattainable women."

"So instead of confronting him, you what? Let him learn his lesson the hard way?" Diarmuid's tone was flat, and the druid admired his self control. "That protection spell you placed on the queen can outwit even the strongest vampyr, and the creatures must feed."

"You're right. Perhaps it wasn't my most compassionate moment. But I didn't think he would conjure an incubus. I thought he would do something foolish like challenge either her next lover, or mine, to a fight to the death. A fitting sacrifice to the Morrigan," she sighed again, and Diarmuid was very hard pressed to stifle the loathing that rose up within him. "But alas, I fear his ire was greater than I originally thought."

"So now what? Are you just going to let the incubus suck him dry, instead of your mistress?"

"I could," and the coldness in her violet eyes rendered them more hideous than anything Diarmuid had ever seen, "but, hero, you remind me my queen is mortal and that I owe her fealty. And that makes me equal to all her other vassals, including this one. I will deal with the incubus, and I will see to it that the creature's master no longer has reason nor power to desire such vengeance again."

He thought about denying her, about confronting the queen and finding out who this man was so he could seek him out and restore his sanity if possible, and relieve him from the temptation and weakness of mortality if not. But he knew, as the druid watched him with her coy smile, that he had neither the power nor the wisdom to navigate this labyrinth on his own.

So he smiled, and he bowed, and he walked away.

—

"That was fast. Convenient, too, as I have a new ritual I want to try and it involves both you and a full moon and-"

"Miri," he interrupted her. "Have *you* slept with the queen?"

Her eyes danced, and she smiled her slow, playful smile again. "Are you sure you want the answer to that question, Diarmuid?"

He paused.

"No. No, actually, I don't."

V

BELTANE

Beltane. A long ivory pole, its cap bedecked in flowers and trimmed in long strands of woven cord, stood out from the otherwise muddy and featureless wood houses. Flocks of sheep grazed with unwonted freedom on the hillside while their shepherds were busy elsewhere with lightskirted paramours. Most would at least hide among the trees, or in stacks of fresh hay piled in the long peat brick pens built between the village and the farms.

Some liked the graveyard. Qimmirea spent most of her afternoons chasing them out with her broom.

"Come now Miri. What better way to celebrate death than by creating life?" heckled Diarmuid from the hearth where he sat idly scraping his knife with a whetstone and crunching a bright red apple.

"Go sweep something. There's dirt everywhere," sighed Miri, shaking a finger at him.

"You took the broom. Again. Can't you at least act the proper witch and use your wand?"

It hung above the fireplace. A single thread of spider's silk wound from it to the mantle. Diarmuid brushed the thread away, careful not to touch the glistening rod or the sheaf of dried wheat, woven with yarn, that draped from it.

"Pfft. You don't want to know when the last time was I used that thing. Now here's your broom. Make yourself useful, and I'll see you at the Maypole."

She vanished into her quarters, humming a simple ditty that started bawdy and ended lewdly enough to make even Diarmuid's ears burn. He shook his head with a smile and began sweeping.

When next he saw her she stood between Aisla and Gerthe, another daughter of Gewinna. Her ruddy head came up to the willowy women's shoulders. Though not in the first blush of youth, she held herself with dignity, and Diarmuid barely noticed the more conventional beauty of the maids beside her. Robed in a loose cotton kirtle in spotless white, she had girdled her plump waist with a cord woven of gold threads and glass beads that sparkled in the spring sunshine. As always, she walked barefoot, and wore no jewelry but the belt and a crown of henbane.

But it wasn't her raiment that drew his attention. It was her radiant, dazzling smile - a smile he'd sometimes caught brief glimpses of, but seemed always to vanish quickly. Aisla leaned in and whispered something into her ear and she laughed, loud and lively. Her laugh, a bark-like sound, may not have been particularly melodious. But it came from her whole being and filled every line of her posture, crinkling the bridge of her nose and throwing back the chest often caved in on itself in anxiety or concentration.

A knot of little children, tumbling over each other like a rough litter of puppies, ran for the Maypole. They clutched reed baskets full of flower petals which they tossed pell mell into the air, onto the dirt, into each other's faces. Music accompanied the limpid sounds of their youthful laughter. Ruddy faced youths grabbed the hands of lily maids and pulled them into a line around the maypole, dancing and, though far from manhood, flirting vivaciously; their youthful innocence aping the mysterious rituals of their elders.

Diarmuid melted into the background amid a knot of surly men whose flowers of youth had long since wilted and who grumbled and griped with one another through the foam of beer on their braided beards. Like him, they danced better with blade than with lass. But even the darkness of war and the horror of facing a thrust of spear, or fang of beast, could not quite dim the brightness that shone on their faces as they watched the village at play.

Beltane. The spring of life. The beginning anew. A lone steer lowed in the distance, led between two bonfires that burned brilliantly at the crossroads. Cloaked figures watched in benediction. Queen Niamh's wandering druids, he guessed, by the long black braids that escaped their hoods and were tucked into fine silver belts around their waists. The farmer leading the steer bowed to the women, then slit the throat of his beast before them.

Beltane. The feast begins.

"Tell me you've had more than just drink, then?"

She slid next to him at the nearly empty long table, pushing a wooden platter of roasted meat into his hands.

"I've not even had much of that," Diarmuid grunted, as he held out his upturned horn from which nary a drop spilled.

"Now that is a tragedy indeed, and explains to me the sour look upon your handsome face," she chided flirtatiously, pouring the contents of a fresh mug into his empty horn.

"Where'd that come from?" He asked helplessly, dazzled still by the grin on her face.

"I asked nicely. Now, *Sláinte,*" she ordered.

With the toast they quaffed their drink. As the spirits began to loosen the tension in Diarmuid's frame he played idly with a piece of meat from the platter.

Qimmirea leaned toward him and opened her mouth suggestively. He rolled his eyes and put the meat on her tongue.

"Have to prove to you I haven't poisoned it, after all," she grinned as she swallowed and helped herself to another piece. "Come now, Diarmuid. Without life there would be no death. Though Beltane is not our goddess' festival, none know its importance better than she."

She elbowed him playfully and held a piece of meat out between her own fingers. He couldn't help but smile, closing his eyes and opening his mouth. The roasted haunch - the sacrificed cattle - melted on his tongue. A gift of death turned into a gift of life. The light of the massive bonfires flickered in her hair, the grease on her lips. He watched her bosom lift slightly as she breathed, and he wondered what it would be like to taste her.

I have always longed for the sweet taste of death.

Suddenly she stood, beckoning him to join her at the Maypole where the older villagers danced with wild abandon. The children had long since succumbed to full bellies and the warmth and exertion of the day, laying soundly asleep in beds of straw. Some of the maids had drawn their lovestruck swains to the darkened hillsides. Niamh's druids lay coupled with men in the light of the fire, crying their devotion to Danu, the Earth Mother, who superseded even their beloved Morrigan. Diarmuid noticed Aisla swinging blithely around the pole with Fenian, a hale and hearty youth who'd often shadowed the warrior around the village, her yellow locks draped with the flowery crown of the May Queen. Gerthe leaned tipsily between two men, one of whom had a hand halfway up her skirt.

"Our women know their power here," assured Qimmirea. And certainly there seemed to Diarmuid no reason to fear lust turning to violence. The village hummed with joy, vivacity; the moans of ecstasy on the wind thanksgiving for another winter passed by, another summer hard won. He caught Qimmirea looking at him from the corner of her eye.

"Do you partake of these rituals too?" He asked huskily, not quite able to make the question sound natural. She laughed, grabbing his hand. Her palms were warm.

"Of course. But am I going to make you my conduit, when you look a squeamish virgin on the first night he gains his manhood? Absolutely not."

"I'm no squeamish virgin, Miri," The accusation chased away his embarrassment, just as she'd intended. "I could make you scream so loud it would put these bleating sheep to shame."

"Is that an offer?"

"Would you accept?"

She studied him for a moment. The rest of the tension had released from his frame. The horn tucked into his belt had been empty for some time. A fire burned in his eyes, and not just in reflection of the ones around them.

"I'd be lying if I said no. But the night is young, and we've been dancing around one another like wary wolves for so long I've not quite got used to the idea of bedding you just yet. Come dance with me, and then maybe I'll make you help me sing a song to the Morrigan."

He kept her hand in his. Though her hands had so often touched death, much like his had, there was a warmth to them he desired. His voice carried alongside hers, low, grave, surprisingly tuneful. Niamh's druids, their bare skin glowing like moonlight, sang too.

The gods were listening. They sang their hearts out, after all.

A shower of stars met the horizon. An omen, for ill or good only the future could tell. They followed the path of the slain steer, stepping through the puddle of his blood, leaping over the ashes. The bonfires at the crossroads had burned down to smouldering heaps full of brands glowing with the runes of the old gods. The flowers wilted on the Maypole.

He swept her over the threshold and laid her gently on the altar. Her hair spilled out of their braids, lighting their own kind of fire at the stone feet of the goddess. He gently unknotted the girdle at her waist, enjoying the sound the beads made as she coiled them gently next to a metal singing bowl.

The lacing of his own trousers came apart just as easily in her nimble fingers. She pulled him free, stroking softly, letting her calloused fingertips linger against him as he felt himself harden with her touch. A ritual for the goddess, whose stone features watched from above, guarding them, protecting them. He slid a hand up her skirt, sighing almost imperceptibly in relief as he discovered she wore no underclothes. His sigh did not go unnoticed. She giggled and shimmied closer to him, and he cupped his fingers around her chin and kissed her forehead, softly, gently.

She met his every stroke. A gentle thrust of blade between ribcage, a hammer on the anvil. Like he promised, she screamed his name so loudly the rafters seemed to ring. He felt a fire within him he didn't recognize, a desperate longing as she shivered in ecstasy below him. Like magnets were his fingers drawn to the soft flesh of her hips, pulling her closer to him; as close as she could get. She wrapped her thighs around his waist without the hesitation they had felt in each other's presence for so long now. He pushed his tongue between her teeth and stroked the softness that parted around him with rough, but dexterous fingers. A smile curled his lips as she moaned in his mouth, unable to control the sounds of pleasure he drew from her even as he too lost himself in the sensation of her warmth, her eager pull at his entire essence. At some point she reached back and grabbed the idol, bracing herself against it to find greater purchase for every measured thrust. And he met her fervor with passion, matching hers with his own. The light of the Morrigan was in her eyes. But all he saw were their painted indigo hues, the crow's feet that crinkled at their corners as she smiled and sighed in pleasure; the sheen of sweat on her brow, her ruddy cheeks, her parted lips. How could he think of death with her taste on his tongue, her hands in his hair, her breath on his neck? What goddess did he bless as he moaned her name in her ear?

"Miri, I want..."

"Don't ask. I know."

He released inside her. It felt like dying. He still had yet to know what dying truly felt like, but this had to be close. Nothing mattered but that single moment as she cried out with him, their voices blended in a prayer to the goddess. Her shuddering thighs pressed against his, both bruised and slick with sweat. Candles wavered in the wind of their shared exhales, the triumphant sigh of success.

He slid out from between her legs and laid down beside her, winding his fingers in her hair. She snuggled into his chest, drawing patterns in the goosebumps and scars on his flesh. He could feel the runes she drew. *Ingwaz, Wunjo, Fehu.* The gods believe in human strength. They walk among us like they wish they were of us. Badb's amethyst eyes glisten in the crowd. The Dagda watches with the old warriors. Brigid holds her sheaf of wheat, smiling knowingly, sweetly, sadly.

The Morrigan has not called for you, hero.

But she *has. I hear my name on her lips, ringing in the rafters.*

—

He woke slowly the next morning, the murky light of dawn making its way through the window to shine on his face. She slept still beside him, her lips parted slightly, her hair damp. He could tell the arduous rituals of the day before had taken its toll and he slowly disentangled himself so as not to disturb her slumber.

Washing quickly in the brook behind the oratory, the chill of its icy waters refreshed and reinvigorated him. On the hills shepherds were already driving their sheep, eager to let the heat of summer aide their flock and the gods bless them with bounty. The pastoral scene seemed almost too charming for words.

Turning back to the shaded oratory, he spotted Miri just beginning to stir, rubbing her eyes and blinking at the light coming through the window. He smiled despite himself.

"You rise late, priestess," he teased. "The day is already half gone."

"Chide me not, Diarmuid," she mumbled, cradling her head in her open palm as she yawned widely. "I am no shepherd. What need have I to waken early?"

She stretched like a cat, arching her back out of the cocoon of furs and blankets. Yawning again, she narrowed her eyes in an attempt to focus on him as he leaned on the doorframe, a silhouette against the late morning sun.

"Surprised you've stayed, if I'm honest," she said with a lopsided grin. "Is not it the custom for men to disappear once they've finally bedded their woman?"

"I like it here," he replied simply, with a smirk. "Or did you expect me to follow Niamh's druids back to Arbannen Castle?"

"They invited you?"

"In no uncertain terms," he swallowed uncomfortably, remembering the glitter in the druids' eyes as they seemed to devour every inch of his body where he stood. She laughed.

"Aye, and you think I'm to protect you from them,
then? You've too much faith in me, warrior. It has never
occurred to them to leave my heroes alone before. What
is mine is simply that which they have not yet decided to
want yet. You watch yourself."

"I serve only the one mistress, Miri. I think it more than
enough to draw upon the blessings of only one of her
priestesses. Am not so greedy as to need the power of
more than that."

"Hmm. I think I will take that as a compliment," she
replied.

"You should."

"Flatterer! Come now, I admit you know very well what
you're about," she said, shivering lasciviously in a way
that stirred Diarmuid's loins. "And the goddess heard
you clearly, that is absolutely for certain. But you owe me
nothing, and I expect even less."

He knelt by the couch, so that she could see the depths
of honesty in his piercing blue gaze. She blushed. "If you
want me to leave, I will leave," he said simply, reaching
a hand to stroke a finger lightly against her blooming
cheek. "Until then, and not a moment sooner, I promise
I will stay. I like it here," he said again, with earnest and
heartfelt sincerity, "and I trust the hands in which my
goddess left me."

He grabbed them, lacing his fingers through hers and
feeling again the warmth in her palms. She squeezed him
lightly, and for a moment they sat in silence, enjoying the
dance of motes of dust that reflected the light through the
window.

The bleating of sheep on the hillside drew them from their reverie. She stretched and stood to dress, while he repaired to the kitchen to break his fast on the bannocks that rose on the hearth and sent forth their savory aroma. He watched her wrap her hair into a soft hood, tucking it back from her forehead and out of her way as she began to tidy the altar.

There was something soothing in the peace of the domestic scene. Though the heart in his chest beat for war, and battle, and the strife of the strength of man against all that would stand in his way, he began to understand a little what drew these villagers to their quiet homes and easy way of life. A heady smell of incense caught his attention and, juggling the fried bread in his hands to cool it, he removed from the kitchen to where she stood at the altar.

She prays quietly, her bare feet tucked beneath her, one hand clutching the slowly burning stick of resin and the other rolling a handful of bones with runes carved into their smooth surface. He watches as she tosses them, reading the prophecies they cast under her breath, shaking her head at some and shrugging her shoulders at others. She moves swiftly, as though they held their own in conversation, speaking through them in a language he barely recognizes. He is entranced, watching her, and he admires the confidence she radiates, the surety he recognizes in her as she kneels at the feet of her beloved deity. Like the quiet before the battle, the calm that settles into him as he approaches mortal danger, he knows the clarity with which she hears the Lady's coveted call.

Without disturbing her he disappeared into the graveyard, idly regarding the smooth stones that mark those who lay in the earth beneath them. As he did so he stumbled across Aisla, who knelt beside a simple stone marker with her hands full of flowers.

"Apologies. I don't mean to disturb," he said, raising his hands in pardon.

"You disturb me not, hero," she said with a charming smile. She stood and dusted off her skirts, leaving the flowers on the stone.

"Your family?" He asked.

"What remains of them," she said with a faint sigh. "Gewinna and her warriors couldn't carry all the bodies so far. She had the dead of my village all burned upon a single pyre so their bones would be desecrated by neither animal nor man. I went back some time ago and collected the ashes that remained to bury them here, that I might always be close to them and not forget the home from which I came."

The breeze tousled her long golden hair, which she wore loose and uncovered. She looked different to all the villagers; more akin to the beautiful Brynhilde for whom he'd fought not long ago. He wondered who she had been before, but realized with a start that it truly mattered not. She, like him, had found a new life in Eillear.

She seemed to follow his trail of thought, smiling kindly and extending a hand. "I am glad to be here. I regret it not that instead of death, the Morrigan chose to guide me to new life among these people. I am glad to see that you, perhaps, feel the same."

"I do." His eyes drifted toward the stone oratory. "The goddess has no use for regret. And if there is still need of my spear, I am proud, and pleased, to put it to use in defense of her devout followers."

"Forgive me for being so bold. You have no home? No family?"

"No need for forgiveness; I am not offended. No."

"So strange. You look like the people of this land. You must not come from afar?"

"I do not. The valley from which I hail is much like this one. Though it, like your own village, was laid to waste not so long ago."

"I'm sorry," she said simply, but he felt her sincerity and smiled.

"I did not lose so much as you. I was young when apprenticed to a blacksmith far from my home, and he soon became the only family I knew. It was no great loss, and it brought me to the path of the Morrigan. I cannot begrudge such a destiny. I would feel the loss of this home with greater poignancy than the one which I left," and he winced, a haunted expression suddenly darkening his brow.

She missed it, and continued on blithely. "We are honored by your presence here. And it is welcome for as long as it cares to be."

He shook himself and bowed, saying nothing. She continued on her way, passing out of the graveyard and back to the village below. He watched her go, appreciating the elasticity of her step and the way she rose from the ashes of her immolated youth to greet this new future promised her.

And so passed Beltane, the beginning anew.

VI

SPEAR OF THE HUNT

The changing of the season came and went, the budding leaves on the trees blooming one by one and spread like an emerald screen over the slow moving river. Those who lay buried upon its banks slept soundly, soothed by the lullaby of softly lapping waves on the Fyroe's pebbly shores.

The sound of winding horns carried up the hill and into the woods, echoing faintly in the chambers of the little oratory.

"Ooh. A hunt, you say?" Miri, busy with lighting a cone of incense on the altar, turned to regard Diarmuid with interest.

"Yes. The king's men have spotted a giant boar in the forest."

"Again?" Miri mumbled under her breath, before rolling her shoulders and smiling. "Well. A fine hunt to you, then, and may the Lady let your bow and spear fly true."

He nodded gracefully. Even her most flippant blessings carried weight. "Were I to bring you an offering, have you any specific requests?"

"Hmm. A hare, if you please, nothing more."

He was too busy being offended to observe the cheeky

grin that bloomed upon her face. "You doubt my hunting abilities?" He scoffed, her measly request raising his ire.

"What use have I for a boar? The villagers have cleaned me out of talismans, and I'll always need pelts. Soothe thy wounded pride and save your puffed chest for the hunters."

Her mischievous and playful smile disarmed reproach. With a sigh and a grin of his own, he took his spear and followed the sonorous call of the hunter's horns.

King Hrothgir himself hailed Diarmuid's approach, dismounting his horse and clapping the warrior on the back with a mighty hand.

"Diarmuid! So Miri cut her apron strings once more; all the better for our hunt. You mount beside me," he commanded, and leapt upon the back of his fiery black steed as one of his men led a dappled silver hunter up to the warrior.

"With pleasure. And Darothil?" asked Diarmuid, peering into the small knot of hunters, whose mounts were pawing and stamping in anticipation. Conspicuously absent from among them was the prince: Hrothgir's son, Darothil.

"The lad couldnae be bothered to wait, and rode off as soon as he heard tell of the beast. We'll find him, upside down in a ditch or trampled beneath the boar's hooves, I'm sure."

Diarmuid winced. "Darothil is a splendid hunter, and a mighty warrior."

The elder warriors snickered amongst themselves, and

Hrothgir cast Diarmuid a derisive look. "Hmph. Don't let him hear you say that. His head's swollen enough as it is. Come!" And with another winding cry, the hunt headed out to the forest, deep into the wildest thickets where roamed the ancient beasts of yore.

As the legends told it, in the forest dwelt a great boar, who stood as tall as a man and as wide as a bale of hay. The beast bore not two horns, but three; two tusks of yellowed ivory that curled from its teeth, and another that jutted from the peak of its massive forehead. As it ran, it split the earth, and could fell a tree with a single charge. Such a beast should be easy to find, thought Diarmuid, in this still and quiet wood. But so far the loudest beings in it were themselves.

"Hark! I spot Darothil," rasped a hunter, winding her horn in greeting. The lone horseman rode up, pulling on the reins of a tawny red horse.

"Any tidings of the beast?" asked Diarmuid, as he nodded deferentially to the king's son.

Darothil curled his lip ever so faintly, but nodded in return. "I have found the boar's trail. Further off in yonder woods, the earth is cracked and trees bowed and broken as though struck by bolts of lightning. It leads deep into the thickest of the forest; I know not if our steeds will manage the narrow tracks."

"We will ride until the forest pass forces us to foot," declared Hrothgir, cutting Darothil off summarily. The prince narrowed his eyes and subsided, bowing in deference to the king.

They swept off, following the trail marked by Darothil, hearty and hale with the promise of the hunt. The heart-

shaped hinds of doe and stag disappeared in the gloom
before them, and foxes slunk away into the undergrowth,
wary of hunters and their dogs who bayed ceaselessly
and snapped their frothed maws. Spotting many a
bounding rabbit, Diarmuid waited for an opportunity
when he was least watched, then let fly an arrow or
two from the bow slung over his back. King Hrothgir
noticed him tying the brace of hares to his pommel, but
graciously made no comment. A glint of amusement
passed in the king's eyes, and Diarmuid recalled the mark
of recognition he made when the warrior mentioned
living with Miri, the priestess in the Eillear forest.
He wondered what Hrothgir knew of the mysterious
priestess, but the he held too much respect for the king to
question the man too closely.

"Hark! The boar's passage is marked!" cried a hunter,
who had paced ahead of the group and just now circled
back. "What the prince says is true. Clearly the beast has
penetrated the very deeps of the ancient forest, where
even the most sure-footed steed would falter."

The king harrumphed under his breath, but dismounted
without further conflict. The rest of the hunters did the
same and, following the broken ground that marked the
massive hooves of the fearsome beast, plunged into the
dark and tightly packed foliage of the inner forest.

Diarmuid perceived the difference between the bright,
lively wood they originally traversed and the dense,
ancient darkness of this one almost instantly. He knew
beyond a shadow of a doubt that the gods walked
here - that beings beyond mortal comprehension made
their home in this, the last bastion of the old world; the
stronghold of the fae, whose mischief and power now
existed only as legends among the hardy and worldly
human folk of Eire. And he could sense the closeness of

his goddess; as he walked with King Hrothgir, rearguard to his massive frame, her voice grew very clear indeed.

What danger have we stumbled upon, he wondered to himself, clutching his spear and balancing effortlessly on the balls of his feet. As they pushed further into the gloom, he became hard-pressed to view even the king's broad back ahead of him. The rest of the hunters vanished completely. Only an occasional voice or crack of twig underfoot recalled him to the presence of other men.

"Diarmuid."

The king had stopped in the middle of the path. As Diarmuid approached, he understood why. Before them, an immense oak had fallen across it, brought down by a great force. Embedded in its trunk were bristles from a boar, and gleaming sap dripped from a gash, three strokes, that cut deep into the bark.

"The men will have circled around by now. We must press on; find the trail again on the other side," Hrothgir said, gripping the ridges in the coarse bark and pulling himself up. Diarmuid followed, both scaling the bole of the fallen tree with ease.

They stood atop it, peering into the distance. Before them lay a pool, dappled by light from the thinning trees above. And at the edge of the pool, with its snout disturbing the tranquility of the waters, stood a tremendous boar - larger even than the legends told. From either side of its mouth curled the two long ivory tusks, and there, from the center of its head between its beady red eyes, protruded the third.

"He's real. Gods preserve us, the beast is true," breathed Hrothgir.

"True, and dangerous. How mean you to face such a fiend?" hissed Diarmuid under his breath. No man on Earth could face this foe and find victory, he knew within an instant.

"With my axe, and your spear, of course," the king replied with a cocky grin. He leapt from the trunk and landed nimbly on the path, Diarmuid following uncertainly. He hoped the other hunters would find them quickly, but he wouldn't abandon Hrothgir to face the boar alone. Then he grinned ruefully, as he caught himself judging that reckless behavior he himself often exhibited.

I suppose I owe Miri an apology. Or, at least something more than a pitiful rabbit.

As they began to approach the clearing in which the pool stood, Diarmuid noticed the trail branched off in either direction around it. He saw King Hrothgir examining the fork in the path, and sighed under his breath when he realized exactly what the king intended.

"You want us to split up, don't you," he groaned in response to the king's delighted expression.

"Come now, you look a judgmental old woman," chided Hrothgir, as he shouldered his axe with a grin. "The boar can pick only one of us to charge, and the other can surprise it in the meantime. Take the left, and I shall go right."

Without waiting for Diarmuid to argue, he swung about and took off down the path. Diarmuid simply sighed again and turned down the other, hoping he could move more swiftly than the eager king.

Whispers, the moaning of ancient and mythical beings as they spoke in tongues understood by no mortal man, surrounded him as he plunged the depths of the murky forest. Otherwise, the wood was deathly still. He wondered where the rest of the hunters had gone; he wondered if perhaps he and Hrothgir had stumbled into a miasma that marked a passage between this world and the next. They seemed to be alone. They two against the great beast, who belonged neither to the world of mortals nor the ethereal home of the gods.

Finally, through the trees, he caught sight of the king rushing up the side of the pool with axe in hand. The boar, who originally seemed to take no notice, suddenly pivoted and snorted, letting out a fearsome cry that shook the very leaves of the trees above them.

But Hrothgir feared not the fiend's hellish scream. He let loose one of his own, a war cry that echoed throughout the misty wood. They charged one another and Diarmuid waited with bated breath, his spear drawn back, for the opportunity to strike and fell the beast.

The ground began to tremble. The boar stamped and snorted, unleashing his fury and causing the earth to wobble and crack. In an instant, Diarmuid watched in horror as the ground beneath Hrothgir's feet disintegrated and Hrothgir, unable to balance himself on the shifting path, pitched forward and stumbled in his mad career.

The very air seemed to flee from Diarmuid's lungs. Without hesitating he bent down and scooped up a sharp rock, flinging it with all his might at the charging monster.

The missile struck true. The boar, knocked from its dash, shook its head and screeched again, then turned the fire of its fiendish gaze upon Diarmuid. Again the earth began to quake, and again the beast charged, straight toward the lone warrior.

The forest whispered with the words of the old gods. But though Diarmuid strained to hear the call of one, she remained silent. No mournful tune accompanied the thundering hooves, no beating wings of ravens on high to claim his soul for the Morrigan. He clutched his spear with knuckles white. Then, at the last possible second, he hurled it with all his might at the beast that bore him down.

Then all went black.

When next he woke, he could see the colourful shards of glass that hung above the altar in Miri's cozy oratory, reflecting their blue and emerald hues on the face of the stone idol. Through a haze of herbs meant to sedate him and the cool dim light of the shaded windows, he saw two figures seated nearby. Miri hovered cautiously over his couch, and King Hrothgir sat erect beside the hearth. They both spoke in low tones, but as he struggled to consciousness their words became more clear.

"…lucky bastard. What I wouldn't give to be tended by a comely lass again," spoke the king from the fireside.

"Lucky? Hrothgir, he's nearly lost his leg. And while I have reason to doubt his powers of self-preservation, I'm almost certain it was in defense of someone else. I'm assuming you, since you're the one who brought him here."

The king chuffed under his breath. "Tis not a mortal

wound, Miri. He'll recover. But I owe him gratitude, and perhaps my life, that is true."

"'Perhaps' your life. Your ear grows deaf to the call of the Morrigan, O great king, but call she does. And one day, it will be for you," Miri warned, subconsciously stroking the furs that lay atop the motionless warrior.

The king snorted, laughing and leaning forward to slap her thigh. "Reminds you of me, does he?"

"You were never half so reckless," she sighed in exasperation.

"I was worse and ye know it. You've gone hard in your old age, Miri; I don't recommend it," he replied soberly, "though ye look the same as ever ye did."

She smiled coyly, then sighed. "I'm tired of heroes, Hrothgir. They come and they go, they call on me and then, they die."

He looked at her pensively, the wise wrinkles on his face for once not marred by bluster or bluff. "You're so used to being the one giving help you've simply forgotten how to ask for it. But you asked not for my advice, so I'll give ye none."

"That's a first."

He chuckled under his breath, and squeezed her thigh again before rising to leave. She too stood and bowed.

"Bless you, King Hrothgir. May the Lady be with you as you go."

As he left, her eyes were sad. She noticed Diarmuid

watching from the couch, and turned to kneel beside him.

"You're awake, then?"

"Yes."

"And you heard me?"

"Every word."

"Diarmuid," she sighed, pinching the bridge of her nose with her fingers. He waited for her to apologize, or explain herself. But her next words surprised him.

"Do you know the tale of how Hrothgir became king?"

He didn't respond, but couldn't resist looking at her with interest. She took his silence as assent and continued.

"Hrothgir was the youngest son of Lugh, one of the greatest chiefs to ever live in the land of Eire. The youngest son of five sons, each as renowned in bravery and might as the other. Do you have any idea what it's like to grow up in that kind of shadow?"

He knew she didn't expect a response, so he didn't offer one.

"Hrothgir was apprenticed to a shipwright. He would carve the ships and then, one by one, watch as his brothers sailed off in them to lands beyond, returning laden with gold and treasure beyond compare. It went so until Hrothgir came of age, and his father went to battle with his elder sons beside him."

Her eyes grew misty. "Lugh was... a legend. A wonderful and righteous king. For as long as he ruled, peace and plenty were known in Bjirtka and all the surrounding lands of the Eire. But he, like all men, grew old. And he knew he must pass this mantle to one of his sons."

"You speak as if you... knew him," queried Diarmuid cautiously. Miri smiled her slow, mysterious smile.

"Perhaps I did. But it matters not. Lugh was slain in battle - he heard the Morrigan's call, and the ravens flew his soul on wings of black to Tir na nOg. He was dealt a mortal wound, and on the battlefield where he drew his final breath he called his four sons to him. All but Hrothgir, who worked in the shipyard still.

"'It is my solemn wish,' he said as he lay dying, 'that my lands pass to my blood, and that they remain in hands as capable and as just as mine have been. I am not a perfect king, and among you, my sons, there is no perfect heir. But I have chosen.'

"He closed his eyes, and with his final breath, he spoke a name: 'Hrothgir.'

"Now, none of his four elder sons expected that. Nor did they intend to honor it. They each meant to be king, and perhaps expected that they would split the kingdom amongst themselves, each to rule in their own right. But their youngest brother, the simple shipwright, had no claim to the throne; or so they thought. They realized they must come to an agreement and elect amongst themselves one to claim as heir, and hide the truth of their father's intent."

"So then... how came you to know the king?" Diarmuid asked, as she paused for breath.

She smiled again. "Hrothgir had a vision. In a dream, a

bright and beaming girl-child came to him and tossed white lilies into his lap. When he bent and asked her name she bowed and cried 'Hail to the great King!' He awoke, and knew not the import of his dream, and so chased it from his mind and returned to the shipyard. The next night, he dreamed again; this time of a beautiful woman with raven hair and belly round with child. She too smiled and handed him a bouquet of white lilies before bowing and declaring, 'Hail to the mighty King!' He woke, and wondered, though the next day no tidings had come. And finally, as he slept that third night, a third dream came upon him. A wizened old woman, whose eyes had seen the fullness of life and now waited patiently for the greatness of death, approached him and laid an armful of white lilies at his feet. Before he could ask for her name she bowed, and whispered only, 'Hail to the just King!' And then, he woke."

"The maiden, the mother, the crone," muttered Diarmuid with a crooked smile.

"That is what he thought as well. So he sought a *bean feasa*, a priestess who could tell him of his dream and who could guide him to seek the fortune it promised. For he grew up in the shadow of a great father, and four brothers, and so had always thought himself unworthy."

"Miri. How old are you?" Diarmuid asked quizzically. She scoffed in mock anger.

"How dare you! And I thought ye a warrior of kindness and tact. Besides, this isn't about me. This is about Hrothgir."

Diarmuid searched her face with knitted brows. Her face was fresh and bright, her form, though small and round, still bore the elasticity of youth and vigor. He wouldn't put her age much above thirty. Yet here she spoke about the youth of an aged king and the reign of a generation before even he. But he put up his hands apologetically and she continued her tale.

"Anyway, he found one. A witch living in the outskirts of the Eillear woods who served the Morrigan, the Goddess of death and Chooser of the slain in battle. Our great Lady who so shapes and fulfills our fate and our destiny. And though his brothers returned bearing upon their shields the lifeless body of his father, the great king Lugh, and though the eldest claimed himself the heir of Lugh and Lugh's kingdom, the wise woman knew the truth. She spoke to Lugh beyond the veil; the soul of the slain king, who could not rest until his sons honored his final words."

She sighed quietly, and wiped a furtive tear from the corner of her eye. "This story does not have a happy ending, Diarmuid. Lugh came from a line of warriors, kings who earned their throne by bathing it in the blood of their enemies. Hrothgir is no different. He grew up the youngest son, a simple shipwright in the shadow of brothers who were mighty warriors, and so he too had to earn the throne his father had left to him. He slew his brothers one by one, challenging them to honorable combat, but a battle to the death nonetheless. The Morrigan called for them all, one after the other. And though he knew they left him with no other choice, fratricide is not an easy burden to bear. Hrothgir has since been a wonderful king, a compassionate and powerful ruler who honors the name of his father," she said, and Diarmuid realized anew the strength of her convictions, and the true honor that came with earning her respect, "but he knows the Morrigan one day will call on him, and call for him to atone. We can only hope his greatness is weighed in the balance of his guilt and that he is not left wanting."

The Morrigan has many heroes. Diarmuid knew the truth
of what she'd said. He sighed, forgiving her for her harsh
earlier words, and sought her hand beneath the furs.

"I'm sorry for how I spoke," she said anyways, her
kind and earnest smile once again lighting up her face.
"Your path is your own, and I should not hold you
accountable for the fact it has crossed with mine. I can
even be thankful... yes," she said, as she regarded the pale
warrior, with his dark gold hair spilling across the pillows
and his icy blue eyes fixed on her own.

"I am, indeed, very thankful."

VII

DRAGON'S SCALE

A dragon. They said there was a dragon here.

Well, the smoke that rose from the volcano's caldera certainly seemed dragonish. But it was very much a volcano, and very much not a dragon.

Diarmuid shook his head as he surveyed the scene. *Stealing treasure and livestock... More like the treasure's gone to the bottom of whiskey barrels and the livestock lost to drunken shepherds. But a dragon quest calls for dragon scale...*

A bright glimmer caught his eye. He wiped the sweat from his brow and knelt, dusting ash and gravel from a shiny piece of obsidian. Its oilslick surface glistened mysteriously, and he could see other, similar razor sharp shards scattered haphazardly across the thin ridge that ran around the mountain's gaping maw.

Dragonscale. She'll laugh me out of town, but the rest of them won't know better, and... He peered through the gloom and noxious gases, shrugging with a noble grin. "Should I fall into these pits, surely 'twould be an end most fitting for a hero; disappearing down the gullet of a fiendish dragon."

As he dexterously maneuvered along the narrow ledges, he noticed the ground began to tremble and shake. He braced himself against each tremor, but none proved jarring enough to pitch him headfirst into the steaming black pit. They were, however, jarring enough for him to realize that perhaps a dragon would be the least of Queen Niamh's worries.

If this goes, the entire city will drown in its flow. Is there any way I could...

His gaze lingered on a pile of loose rocks fitted along a ridge that led down the edge of the peak.

Fight a mountain. I'm going to fight a mountain. Morrigan preserve me from your priestess' wrath. If this doesn't kill me, she will.

The mountain made it easy. The large, and very tenuously stacked, chunk of rocky boulders to the north of the caldera seemed to be his best bet at redirecting any pyroclastic flow away from the stone city to the south. Though the boulders easily weighed more than a full grown steer, he managed to leverage a few, and as they began to tumble down the chasm that led away from the mountaintop, the rest begrudgingly followed suit. A few times the mountain even seemed to help him, giving a tremble or a shake when a particularly stubborn rock refused to budge. He began to wonder just how many gods he owed prayers to before the last boulder finally gave way and crashed free.

I can only hope that makes some kind of difference. Won't stop the ash from falling, I'll remember to warn Niamh about that. Or... he stared off in the distance, towards the castle that could still be spotted along the horizon, and wrinkled his nose in distaste, *have someone else warn her.*

For reasons he had yet to explore, he knew he wanted to go straight home. Though he didn't exactly have a need to visit the oratory. Other than sore muscles and a superficial scratch or two, he remained perfectly unscathed from his arduous afternoon. But he knew beyond a doubt the last thing he wanted to deal with right now was Queen Niamh's glittering and suffocating court. As he sighed, rolling back the sleeves of his now tattered tunic, he felt another tremor begin to rock the mountainside. It started slow, a rumble he barely had time to register before his warrior reflexes automatically stabilised him.

Then with an almighty heave and a deafening crack, the ledge he stood upon disintegrated in an explosion of steam and rubble.

He woke in the dark, stiff as a board and unsettlingly numb. A thin plume of ash and smoke disrupted the tranquility of an otherwise clear night sky, encrusted with stars and constellations. He traced three of them. Then he said his name aloud. Then he tried moving his fingers, and toes, slowly, one after the other. The absolute tiniest sensations returned to quiet his fears. As far as he could tell, all his limbs were still attached, and they all, somehow or other, still functioned.

"I think we can chalk that up as a win for the mountain," he said ruefully to himself. He could barely gauge where he'd landed in the dark. But the fact the peak glowed some hundreds of feet above him now indicated that the distance the mountain had thrown him was: far.

Morning graced him with a better understanding of his strength. He could stand, and miraculously, he could even take a few timid steps. The stiffness seemed to linger from his work with the rocks and not from the volcano's eruption. He surmised that since he managed to survive, the shock sustained by his still very mortal body deadened all its other, more severe, effects. There was one very large, and very disturbing, reminder of what exactly happened to him, a mark of proof that he hadn't simply walked down the slopes of his own sweet accord. A massive burn blistered its way from the tips of the fingers on his left hand all the way up to his neck, a wound he was absolutely familiar with from his time in the forge and one he remembered with absolute dread. He had about two days before the shock wore off, and the nerves that now lay dormant under layers of singed flesh would be screaming in agony. So he took a deep breath and pointed his scorched leather boots to the trail leading directly to Eillear.

Soon, sooner than he expected, he found himself staring across the rolling green hills that led toward home. He thought he could see the twisted oaks that shaded the oratory upon its wooded mount. A smile played across his face as he imagined the priestess, on a walk perhaps, staring across the same valley to the peak where he stood. But as he gauged the height of the sun in the sky, he realized it was unlikely she'd be out for a stroll at this hour, for now would be about the time she normally bathed.

He frowned away a blush at that thought.

She marched up the path to the vista on the hillside, the normal harmony of her soul a cacophony of everything that'd gone wrong that day. The oven going out from lack of fuel - and with it, the heat for her bathwater - was simply the final straw of a long day fraught with minor setbacks annoying enough to drive her outside.

If I'm going to bathe late, I might as well work up a sweat to make it worth it, she thought to herself as she stepped gingerly through the soft, clinging mud. The afternoon's settled rain turned the normally smooth trails to a dirty morass, and she began to wonder whether a march through grassier pastures further south would've better suited her purposes.

Of course, she knew exactly why she was heading for the hilltop. From that vantage point, the furthest reaches of the road leading to Eillear could be seen, and along it, any itinerant passersby. Though she tended to expect her heroic housemate to return crippled on the back of a hay cart, she begrudgingly admitted it just as likely he'd simply stroll along the road himself, as though defeating dragons or protecting rulers from violent usurpers or whatever it was Queen Niamh had decided to call upon him for this time were an everyday sort of affair.

But everything that had gone wrong that day could be traced directly back to his absence. And that's what made everything that had gone wrong that day so particularly annoying.

She peered across the valley, to a rocky outcropping that marked the boundary of Eillear's fertile farmland and the more remote regions beyond it. She could, if anyone were around to listen, point out every major marker to the towns that lie in view, state their market days, their prime trade, and every king or war chieftain going back at least a century. Hrothgir of Bjirtka, their own remote king from a well-protected bay to the west. Queen Niamh of Arbannen in her mountain home to the east. And the mystic fens of Odinn's tribe to the north. Since it was on Niamh's behest that Diarmuid had set off this time, Miri's gaze settled eastwards, and though she knew its absurdity, she indulged herself with the idle notion that somewhere in her line of sight his figure could be traced.

Miri, you've lost it. He's probably blankets deep in Niamh's fabled maidens' chamber. They're always looking for able bodies to join their orgies for the gods, and the Morrigan does love a good roll in the hay.

She smiled bemusedly, recalling some memorable rituals of her own, before sighing and shaking her head.

You've always been an easy mistress to please, my lady, she prayed under her breath, her voice mingling with the wind whistling in wet trees. *Guide me now. I can save him for you, if that is your wish. But I know not if I've the strength to save him for... me.*

Like a wraith, he appeared in the gloom of night. She didn't hear him enter - she'd sunk up to her ears in bathwater, closing her eyes like a cat in the sun as the warmth sank into her bones. Which explained why, when she suddenly opened them, they startled each other. He looked away bashfully.

"I didn't hear you in the kitchen, and got nervous when you... didn't answer my knock. I'll just-" he turned in the doorway, but stopped short as she called him back.

"Hand me that robe, if you wouldn't mind," she said, giving a final rinse to her hair before standing up in the bath. She found it almost too easy to be naked around him. For such a virile warrior, he got the cutest blush over the bridge of his nose every time. Cuddling into the robe, she looked him up and down narrowly, inspecting him for the inevitable battle damage he seemed almost always to return with.

Favoring a hand and turning away from the light, he smiled apologetically. "Maybe you should just meet me in the kitchen. I know that look."

"You're hungry too, I see," she responded with a smile, wringing her hair out with a small cloth. "Go on then. I've not eaten yet either, if you'd be so kind."

I guess today stands to end better than it began, she mused to herself as he eagerly stepped out to the kitchen and she remained to dress.

Her optimism vanished instantly as she saw him in the clearer light of the kitchen. "What is... Is that a burn, Diarmuid?"

He hastily shook his sleeve back. "Only a little one!" He replied defensively.

"Put that knife down. A little one he says, with flesh flayed clear to the elbow. And your neck! Come now; you've got some faith in my skill, then, if you expect me to literally save your skin."

As she investigated the wounded warrior more closely, her brow grew darker. "Looks like I've actually got to regrow it. How did you manage to walk a dozen leagues like this?"

The burn extended from the back of his left wrist, up his shoulder, to the side of his neck, with a shock of hair burned black at the base of his skull. In most places the burn was shiny red, but some spots were a dark, mottled black. "You are not going to enjoy this treatment one bit, I hope you're aware of that. Was it a real dragon then? Is this dragon fire?"

My Lady preserve us. Dragons in this enlightened age. I owe the northmen an apology, for thinking them daft drunkards.

He chuckled, wincing slightly. "No. Our dragon was a volcano. A soon-to-be highly active one."

She shooed him away from the hearth fire, bidding him to take a seat at the bench while she pounded a mixture of herbs and tallow in her pestle.

"Go on then, tell me your tale. How long have you had that for?"

"Not long. I woke up at the bottom of the mountain yesterday morning. I knew I didn't have much time before it got too bad for even me to tolerate," he admitted ruefully.

"So you came straight home then? Didn't stop to collect the reward?" She remarked airily, as she measured oils from various vials into the mixture.

He shook his head. "No. I filled a pouch with obsidian shards, and I left them with Fenian on my way here."

"You gave the scales to the Crach's boy? What possessed you to do that?"

"Queen Niamh said the reward goes to whomever brought her proof of the dragon's defeat. She didn't say anything about it having to be the person who actually defeated it in the first place. Besides, what am I going to do with all that obsidian?" He shrugged, then winced as the gesture pulled on his scarred skin.

"You could pay me for your incredibly difficult treatments, for a start," she complained, while beginning to spread the paste along the inside of a shiny brass bowl. Under her breath she muttered prayers of healing, songs she recalled by rote that he could feel the influence of even now.

He rolled his eyes. "Fenian is a smart lad. He'll know how

to play his cards at court. And you've no more use for dragon scale or queenly ransoms than I do, Miri."

She huffed, but didn't argue, and brought the bowl over to where he was seated. She set the bowl in his lap and slowly cut away the remains of the ragged tunic, once they both realized Diarmuid couldn't lift his arms over his head to remove it. The bowl was cool, and seemed to hum with latent magic.

Tears stood in the corners of her eyes as she smoothed the thick paste across his blistered skin. He remained stoic, not wishing to disturb her, until a sniff broke the silence.

"It's the astringent," she insisted, not meeting the glance he cast at her over his shoulder.

"Miri, I'm sorry," he began under his breath.

She slammed her hand down onto the table, rattling the remains of their dinner. "Sorry? For what are you sorry, then?" Her voice nearly shook with anger. "Do you know how many bodies I've buried? Know how many souls I've watched my lady's ravens fly from this world to the next?" She seethed, and nowhere in her voice or eyes was the playfulness Diarmuid had come to recognize. He was shocked. "Do you know the sound a woman makes when her babe is born lifeless, the way men tear their hair when their sons return from war in bags sewn of dirty cloth?"

He hung his head. He knew he owed her the truth. But he didn't even know it, and his ignorance hung heavier on him than the weight of his driving purpose.

"Diarmuid. Look at me."

He did. Her eyes reflected every color of Eire's twilight

sky. When he smelled her, he remembered the taste of victory. Back when victory actually mattered, wasn't just a hollow reminder of his one great failure.

"I don't know what the Morrigan wants of you, any more than you do yourself. I can only imagine why she thought to bring you here, to me, a dirty hedge witch in the middle of the Eillear woods. I could be vain and call it a lesson. I could..."

Admit I'm a one hundred year old reincarnation of the Morrigan herself. No, that would be too easy.

She bit her lip and dissolved into tears, collapsing softly against his bare chest. They filled his own eyes as well, leaked into the firelit locks that tumbled from her braids under his chin. The gods play many games with mortals. Maybe that's why mortals keep making up new gods.

"I don't know why either." *Don't know why I woke up one day in a forge that no longer brought me purpose. Didn't understand the way my blood boiled as the warriors of my tribe returned, glutted with glory dripping from the blades of swords I pounded with my own hands. Watched with inexplicable yearning as the boats bearing our dead floated into the yawning sea, alight with the flames and the ashes of their glorious deeds.*

They held each other close, as though physical proximity could make up for the secrets they locked away from one another.

She is staring at him, a fierce glitter in her eyes that has nothing to do with the drink on the table. He knows, because he accidentally grabbed her mug and didn't realize his mistake until he took a deep draught and tasted only water - she'd reserved her strongest spirits for him, to dull the edge of pain as she mixed up the paste and applied it to his burned flesh.

"I'm thinking you want something, Miri" he says gruffly, as he notices her hand lingering on his chest even after she had used the last of the unguent.

She scoffs, a sound like a bark. Not mocking, but not natural either. "I want many things, Diarmuid. Sometimes I get them, sometimes I don't."

Cryptic - but then again, could the mouth of the gods ever speak in more than riddles? He looks at hers, pursed as it was, biting back words, holding down desire. He reaches for her and she doesn't recoil.

"If the Morrigan gave us to each other," he said, echoing her frustrated sentiments from earlier, "perhaps it is her desires we'd be fulfilling."

He doesn't wait for her to respond. He pulls her up by the shoulders and kisses her, fiercely, leaning forward from his perch on the table to close the distance she keeps between them. Her throat issues a whimper, one she swallows with a breath as he keeps her lips locked to his. But her fingers are in his hair and suddenly it is her backside on the table, not his, and he has both hands up her kirtle to grab her tighter and pull her even closer. Her hips are soft, and firm, and his fingertips find easy purchase in her flesh.

"This isn't the altar," she gasps, with a longing sigh.

"This isn't a ritual." He snarls in her ear, because he is in control of his destiny between her legs and he will not relinquish it for a second.

She exhales, as though unbound as she is unclothed. Her

eyes flash a myriad colors of the sky as day dies, her open mouth a perfect O as he slides himself inside her, burying himself in her soft folds. She feels the scrape of the crisp edge of the drying unguent pressed against his burned flesh, and eyes him with concern for a moment.

He responds by lifting her legs over his hips and thrusting himself even deeper. Pain has never held him back from anything, least of all this.

There are no words they speak. The sounds echoing in the dim and smoky kitchen are her shrieks of pleasure as his body meets hers, stroke for stroke, and his ragged breathing as he consumes her inch by inch. His teeth meet her collarbone, gaining purchase against her flesh as he mounts her, and she cries out and rakes her fingers down his back. Many have tried to break his flesh, and bleed him dry; she does not try.

He loosens his jaw from her throat to aim for a nipple instead, feeling simple joy in the way her body dances against him and the sensation of every shuddering breath she inhales as it flutters in her chest. She has wrapped her legs around his waist, her arms around his head, surrendered completely in a way she could never lose herself to the goddess or to the conduits who have guided her before into the beyond. For this moment, she does not belong to the old ways - to the old gods.

As she cries out, a wave of release spiraling from the crown of her head to the tips of her very toes, she belongs to him. This moment, this coupling, this orgasm he has drawn out of her and everything she has ever felt before or since. It is his, and she controls none of it.

She has never felt more powerful.

The sensation of her contracting around him as she shivers in pleasure pushes him over the edge. He releases inside of her, and though he should be weak from exertion it is a sensation instead of unbridled strength and unparalleled ecstasy. He catches himself smiling - he is even laughing. He buries himself in the crook of her neck, in the curls of her fiery hair, breathing in her scent of sex and incense. And she laughs too in relief at the fire with which they consumed each other.

Perhaps they were a goddess' gift. And perhaps not.

Neither spoke again that night. They didn't need to.

He found her the next morning kneeling at the altar. The sense of peace and tranquility that radiated from her as she communed with their goddess sank into his weary bones. He smiled involuntarily, then slipped out through the kitchen without disturbing her.

He moved stiffly; the paste which she'd applied to his skin hardened overnight into an almost stone-like plaster. Favoring his left arm but moving with purpose, he headed for the icy brook that lay dappled by the morning sun through the trees. While he enjoyed these cold ablutions, he knew she did not, and the least he could do was chop her some more firewood to restore the heat of the oven that lay cold in the corner of the kitchen.

The brook water moved slowly. He could smell the animals that had drunk from it, he could hear the misty waterfall it turned into as it tumbled down the side of their mountaintop. Peace, and tranquility. He had not known what this was. As the icy cold bit his flesh, he realized a life of turmoil and sacrifice is all he knew. All he'd ever known.

I could call it a lesson. If I were vain.

Her words echoed in his head. *Do gods teach lessons? Are we mortals worth the effort?*

As he stood from the water, the paste that had been slowly dissolving began to fall away. He watched it with a worried brow, disturbed by the distinctly black tinge to the otherwise salmon-hued plaster. It hit the water with a plop and dissolved almost instantly, but he determinedly looked away from his burned arm, not willing to remind himself of the extent of the damage. There was every possibility he could never use it again, a very real chance that at any moment, the dull throbbing that had kept him tossing and turning all night would evolve into paralyzing pain.

The last piece fell away. He forced himself to look.

His skin, though perhaps slightly pinker than before, remained otherwise perfectly healed. He drew fingers along his arm, to his elbow; the sensation of touch, sensitive but clear, reverberated everywhere he explored. The clear water, bright with the still dawning light of a morning sun, reflected the smile of relief on his face and the restored smoothness of his neck and shoulder.

"Oh, you didn't have to... well, thank you," she stammered, as he dumped another armful of kindling and split logs into the oven's open grate.

"It's no dragon scale," he said simply, smiling. "But it's the least I can do."

VII

WOLVES AT BAY

Peering into the gloom of the ancient forest, he hears the creak of gnarled and blasted trees. A raven, his Lady's messenger, caws hoarsely at a slowly ambling figure off in the distance. Diarmuid drops to his knees to hide his face in the dirt and dessicated leaves that coat the forest floor.

He feels the figure's single eye, roving, inquisitive, reproachful, pass over his prone form. The bird takes flight and in a shower of iridescent black feathers the figure disappears.

"They are... wolves." Diarmuid recalled the pause in the shepherd's speech and the way his eyes seemed to roll in fear as they regarded the dead sheep. Throat torn by fangs. Belly sliced by knives.

Wolves. They must be wolves.

What else could they be?

"You'll need this," Qimmirea said as she stuffed handfuls of dried herbs into a pouch made from woven cloth. She slapped his hand away as he made to tie it to his belt. "No, don't touch it yet. Not with your bare hands. Until I know what you're made of, that is. Wash them first in this."

He dipped his hands in the bowl she placed before him.

Its waters glittered with flakes of fool's gold and the finest silver dust.

"If I can't touch it," he replied patiently as his fingers dripped water into the bowl, "how am I supposed to use it?"

"You can touch it now, but try to avoid getting your blood on it. They say it's wolves?"

He nodded, wiggling his fingers in hopes they'd dry faster. A fine mist splashed the table. She huffed in annoyance but didn't say anything. From her own neck she took a moonwashed silver pendant and hung it around his. It felt cool against his chest, humming ever so lightly like the tines of a tuning fork.

"If you see any pelts scattered in the forest, burn them. Sprinkle some of this," she patted the pouch tied securely to his leather belt, "on them as they burn. I'm sorry, but you can't leave them even for a moment. You'll have to keep an eye on them until they're completely destroyed."

His nose wrinkled as the ghostly stench of singed fur and flesh filled it. "Oh yes. I do not envy you that task one bit. But it must be done. And don't for a second," she said, turning her stern gaze - the one that made him think she could perhaps see through to the beginnings of his very soul - on him, "think to put the pelt on yourself. That is a curse even I can't lift. Just burn them, for everyone's sake."

"I need no power of shapeshifters," he replied coolly, dexterously flipping his knife in the air. "But thank you for the warning."

No pelts of wolves meet his searching gaze yet. But he

hears their howls. And he smells their bloody breath.

Night falls with a vengeance in the wood. Devilish pixies pass him by, where he kneels in still silence on the forest floor. A single look into that frozen gaze told them they could never sway the warrior, nor break his impenetrable concentration. There are easier targets. One after another all the creatures of the forest leave him alone, regarding him with as much indifference as the moss on the rocks.

The silence grows deafening. A sense of peace rises in Diarmuid's soul even as his other senses heightened to danger and martial vigor. The calm before battle. This is the time his Lady's call could be heard with the most clarity.

Would she call for him this day?

A rustle interrupts the forest's tranquility. Bows of holly and hanging trails of ivy, brushed first by wind, are disturbed now by something larger and more ominous that moves with purpose in the underbrush. The pendant hums against his chest, beats in rhythm to his heart.

Glowing pairs of yellow eyes begin to circle the warrior. But they cannot see him, and so they disperse. He hears them, not too far off, their guttural yelps and fearsome howls subsiding into the clipped speech of men. Their tongue is strange, ancient; but the sour smells of beer and blood are familiar to Diarmuid. He needs only wait til their ferocity leads to gluttony, and that gluttony to stupidity.

They may be wolves. But they first were men.

In early morning, the cat's gloom before day's break, he can see the ragged shapes of their discarded pelts. Six in total litter the floor of the clearing. Without breathing he drags them, two by two, far from their sleeping bearers and deep into a cave in the woods. He moves so swiftly, so silently, they don't stir once, the drink from the night before deepening their stupor.

As he untied the sachet of herbs from his belt he discovered a cloth knotted around it. He shook it out and tied it around his face with a relieved sigh, inhaling the musky scent of incense and sacred oils Miri had doused it in. He wondered if she'd actually given him a discarded altar cloth as he noticed sundry singe marks and a distinct ethereal magic. It couldn't completely protect him from the overwhelming stench of burning hair as he lit the hides in the small, smokey cave, and his eyes watered as he dusted each liberally with the herbs she'd given him. The nettle stung his palms and the wolfsbane left greasy residue between his fingers. But he realized their purpose and his faith in the witch's skill grew. Nettle, so that if the shapeshifters attempted to don the immolated furs they would scratch them off almost immediately, and wolfsbane, that would cause their blood to boil and meat and drink turn to ash in their mouths.

He crouches by the entrance to the cave, knife in hand. In its depths the immolated pelts still smoulder, dwindling into ash. Dawn's light finally penetrates the murky canopy and he knows beyond a doubt the wild warriors will awaken soon and immediately search him out. The pendant begins to pulse again. For a moment, he sees the priestess as she casts her spell; reading the bones as they roll across the cloth and weaving magic into the silver resting in the hollow of her throat. He takes a deep breath, inhaling again the sweet smell of incense.

Along with it comes the sour stench of unwashed bodies, as the fiends begin to descend upon him.

One lunges for his throat. Though he bore the shape of a man, the instincts of a beast consume him in battle. The others circle warily, alert enough to realize a warrior with the daring to steal their pelts had the strength and vigor to defend himself. Diarmuid grapples with the beast, grabbing the jaws that lunged for his throat in one hand and the ragged fingernails that scraped for his cheek in another. He wonders if the man is even armed with a weapon, and simply forgot his lack of fangs and claws. Not waiting to find out, he tears the werewolf's jaw from its hinges, then with a fearsome yell lands a bone shattering blow to his temple.

In an instant, he is beset by two others. These two are cunning. They bear a club and a dagger, and Diarmuid pulls his own knife from its sheath. But they are simply barbarians, and while they try to bear him down with sheer strength, ferocity, and might; he is a warrior. And he knows where best to draw blood, sever the muscles and sinew and reduce strong limbs to limp, useless appendages. The men yelp and try to retreat among the rest of the pack, but Diarmuid dexterously flicks his knife into the back of one and, wresting the club from the hand of the other, delivers a strike so fierce the man's head collapses.

The next two are consumed by rage at the sight of their fallen brethren. Their mouths foam and teeth snap. Again, he wonders if they even know they are men. Broken fingernails in place of sharp claws drag at his flesh and leather armor. The strength of the beast that curses them may bear down foe after foe, regardless if they are in the shape of man or wolf. But this warrior, who listens in vain for the call of the Morrigan, is no easy target. No weak prey willing to succumb to the feral teeth that bite at his flesh and the limbs that flail fruitlessly against his disciplined strikes.

One, into the heart. Another, across the throat. Both slump to the ground beside their defeated kin.

There is but one wolf left. He continues to circle. The pelts are naught but ash, crumbling on the eddies of wind made by the heat of the fire and the chill of the stone cave. This wolf knew well how to chase prey until it tires. But his prey is not sheep. And his prey does not tire. With a final, throaty howl, the shapeshifter turns and flees into the gloom, alone and without the pelt that transformed him from timid man to feral beast. His death, in this wood where roam creatures of fearsome strength and vicious nature, is assured.

Diarmuid debated following him, bringing him a swifter end, a more complete justice. But he felt blood pouring from his cheek where ragged teeth met his flesh and dull pain radiating from where a strike from the club landed true on his ribs. The smell from the cave became nauseating. The altar cloth tied around his face now lay crumpled on the ground where it had fallen in the heat of battle. He picked it up and gently folded it, tucking it into the empty pouch on his belt.

The ravens watch as he leaves the forest. He dips his head in salute and they fly away. They did not come for his soul today. For an odd moment, as he presses the silver pendant to his heart, he is thankful.

—

"You didn't have to bring the cloth back, but I appreciate it all the same."

She dipped it in a bowl of sweet-smelling unguents,

pressing it gently to the wound on his cheek. He leaned into her hand with a grateful sigh.

"I burned all the pelts, just as you said. I didn't manage to kill off all the men, though." He thought of the eyes, fierce, full of hatred, and yet mournful, of the werewolf who remained. "One wolf did not attack but ran into the forest instead."

"He won't come back. If you destroyed the pelts, it's only a matter of time before he dies anyways. When the next full moon, catching him without the pelt that protects his soul from godly fury, will banish him from Eire and his monstrous soul to Hel. These are curses not easily lifted."

"You said you couldn't lift it, if it fell upon me."

"I did."

"Do you speak truly?" He studied her face as she continued to stroke his cheek softly, humming as she worked. He could feel the flesh begin to knit of its own accord under her hand.

"Are you afraid this bite will turn you to a wolf? You've been listening to the villagers' stories again. No," she said, sucking in a breath and trying not to smile at the softness he couldn't help expressing, "Only betrayal, and a desperate revoking of one's deepest nature, could curse a man to assume the spirit of a beast."

He winced. She apologized, and he realized she thought she'd hurt him with her ministrations.

Shrewd as she is, there are aspects of his nature even she cannot penetrate.

"For your ribs, there's not much I can do since your ability to remain motionless is permanently impaired. Drink this." She held a flask up to his mouth and he drank the sweet spirit infused with feverfew and lavender. A strange concoction, but one he felt the effects of almost instantly.

"I know. Thank you, Miri," he said sincerely, wiping his face with the back of his hand and grasping hers with the other.

"Hmm. Now that's definitely not like you. Perhaps the ravens spoke truly to me after all. Do you need a seance? A ritual with the goddess, perhaps?"

She laid the bloody altar cloth on the table, ignoring the smear of grease from the unguent. He noticed her hands were shaking.

"Do you know why I fear their curse?"

"You don't have to tell me," she replied, shutting her eyes. "There are things men should never have to confess, and I am not your judge. Our Lady knows your heart and she will weigh your worth with justice and mercy."

A worth granted by others. He knew, without speaking, that she wanted him to feel worth of his own. Suddenly he reached his arms out and wrapped them around her, burying his face in the woolen apron she wore over her kirtle. She smelled like incense and baking bread. The softness of her belly felt like home.

"Thank you, Miri."

She smiles.

"Still strange. But, I'll get used to it."

—

He saw his face in the reflection of the burn behind the oratory. The skin torn by the wolf bite had almost completely healed. No wolffish features, save for the slightly elongated canines he'd always possessed, had appeared in the interim. He relaxed in the burn's slow moving waters as it trickled merrily over the rocks and roots of the little wood.

Eillear hummed with quiet joy. Spring had been good to the emerald isle of Eire this year, each day full of a cacophony of birdsong in the morning followed by evenings ringing with the singing of frogs in the marshes that lined the banks of Fyroe. The villages' flock survived the wolf pack and grazed the grassy slopes with fearless confidence.

Diarmuid grew restless. Never did the call of his goddess grow fainter than now, during the season of life; the time of growth and healing from dark and cold winters that gripped this northern land. As a warrior, he had only the strength to struggle and endure. He knew not how to sustain such lethargy, such calm and quiet content.

"I don't know what reckless adventure you're planning now, Diarmuid, but it's clear on your face you're up to no good."

He was practicing with his spear in the graveyard. Its open space and grim silence was as good a place as any for his routine. But at her approach he laid down the weapon and turned to regard her.

"You say that like it's some sort of novelty. No good has

ever come of anything I do," he replied grimly, sneering into the sun as though its light had caused him personal affront.

"If that were any kind of true, you wouldn't have the confidence to admit it," she jibed back. "Just because you pretend to seek that which benefits only you, you cannot act like your actions exist in a vacuum."

"Fine. I save some villagers from monsters and men. I help a princess find a kingly mate. But isn't intent more valuable than the deed? I did those things for a single purpose, and in that purpose, I failed. I can't take responsibility for what that failure caused."

"You can, and you should. The world doesn't owe you anything, Diarmuid. But you do live here, just like the rest of us," she said idly, stroking the chin of a raven whose crimson hued feathers glowed in the sunlight. "Stop acting like you have no duty to live up to others' expectations because you think they don't know you."

"They don't."

"And whose fault is that? You think your sole purpose is to live only to die, whether in some blazing act of glory or in some compelling measure of sacrifice. Has it ever occurred to you for even a moment that you might live, just for the sake of living?"

He was silent. This wasn't an argument he was willing to get into with her. Chiefly because he knew it was an argument he would lose.

"Are you that bored, hero of the Morrigan?" She asked with a crooked smile, seating herself on a stone marker beside him and offering him a draught from the jug she was carrying.

He took a drink, making a face at its sour contents. "Have you some way of occupying my time?"

"Have you ever thought about just taking a nap?"

He glared at her, and she giggled shamelessly. "What? They're refreshing. Give you a new perspective. You should try it sometime. Go lay on a hilltop and let the sun warm you to sleep."

"You're not helping, Miri," he warned, clutching his spear til his knuckles turned white. What could she know of the ache in his breast, the emptiness that only occasionally filled itself with a longing so fierce it threatened to undo him?

Why does she not call for me?

"Everything has to be a struggle for you, else it's not worth having, is that it?" Her tone was light, but he sensed the gravity with which she addressed him.

"Those shapeshifters thought the same. They wanted more than they could have, fought bigger and stronger foes until one day they knew they needed greater strength in order to take on the mightiest. So they thought perhaps they'd dabble in dark magic and call upon the wrong gods for blessings which they understood not. For it turned them against everyone. Not just those they wished to challenge, but their brethren, their lovers, their children, their friends. They acquired great strength, but with it, they lost their humanity - that which sets them apart from beasts and monsters that rove yonder forest. Now they know nothing; not the sweetness of life, nor the honor of death and the glory of an afterlife in Tir na nOg."

She waved laconically, and he flinched as he noted again the scars that ran up her arm.

"Don't pity me, Diarmuid." Her eyes snapped, though her tone was calm. "The Lady brought me back to teach me a lesson, to save me from a similar fate. You'd do well to learn the same. You want to go do something brave, and reckless, and daring? Go find the fae folk that live in the heart of the ancient forest. Tell them you have slain the shapeshifters, for the pelts they wore they stole from the fae long ago. And while you're at it, if they're in a giving mood, beg from them their May ring in return."

"Their... their May ring?" He asked in confusion.

"Yes. At one point the five clans of fae worked in harmony and they made a May ring to bind that harmony to a single source. Clearly they're not using it anymore," and her face grew rather forbidding as she said that, "so I figured it would look good on my altar and maybe imbue some of my rituals with greater strength. Go on. Go do that for me and I'll leave you alone for the rest of the season."

He peered closely at her, his brows knitted in consternation. "Are you... mad at me?"

A sigh escaped her lips. "I've never been mad at anyone in my entire life, Diarmuid. No one is worth my anger," she said very seriously. But without wishing him a fair journey, she simply turned and went back inside the oratory.

Hmm. A visit to the fae folk. He shivered slightly, despite the warmth of the day. Though oftentimes helpful to mortals, most avoided the fae, for they were known to be cunning tricksters who never gave without taking in return. But if Miri was right about the pelts, and the thieves who stole them, then perhaps he had a bargaining chip worth exchanging.

That did not turn out to be the case at all.

She saw him hobbling up the pathway, clutching his shoulder in one hand and the tattered old May ring in the other.

Only the graveyard bore witness to her most heartfelt and piteous expression. But she didn't ask him any questions til she'd seated him at the low kitchen table before the smoking peat fire and done up his arm in a sling and poultice of lavender and willow bark. And she made sure the earthenware mug before him had at least two fingers of strong spirits in it.

"They made me hunt a stag with a sharpened stick, on foot. And then push boulders upstream with my bare hands. And then they made me fight a bear. A bear, I tell you!"

She bit her lip. He couldn't tell if she were trying not to cry, or trying not to laugh. He took a swig from the cup and sighed with a smile, hoping to encourage the latter reaction.

"I wanted to give up. But I thought I must do everything they asked, or else they'd deny me my request."

"It's just a stupid May ring, Diarmuid, I-"

He cut her off, putting up his hand. "No. You were right. I learned my lesson. The challenges would never end.

They would push me and push me till I either tried to attack them or, I don't know, dropped dead I suppose. Each challenge was more dangerous and more reckless than the last. Finally they told me I must walk a length of spider's silk from one treetop to another."

"And?" she said with bated breath.

"I looked at that tree. I looked at the fae, faces in their sleeves as they mocked me with their eyes. And I told them where they could stuff their May ring, for I'd had enough. Even I'm not so reckless," he scoffed under his breath, "as to attempt to walk a thread of spider's silk from one treetop to the next."

She topped off the glass with more liquor. "Then... What did they do?"

"They vanished. Just, poof, right gone. I foiled their trick I guess. They didn't expect a hero to choose to give up. And I suddenly awoke at the edge of the forest, clutching the May ring, surrounded by a fairy circle of toadstools."

The cup made a not-so-violent-but-not-quite-silent-either thud as it tapped the wood of the table. She filled it again.

"Dare I ask... about your arm, then?"

He looked her dead in the eye.

"I tripped."

"Diarmuid. Be serious."

She waited a moment.

"By the goddess, you are serious."

He sighed. He emptied the glass, and then he stood.

"I think I'll go take that nap now."

IX

BLESS THE RAINS

It rained. And it rained. And it rained some more. This was Eire, after all; rain was no exceptional occurrence. But the burn behind the oratory rose ever higher, climbing its banks in disorderly fury, and men built log dykes along the borders of Eillear to prevent the maelstrom that was once the languid Fyroe from washing their long houses away.

This was rain like no other, like no one living had seen before. And so they fled to the hills, to higher and higher ground. And they sent for their priestess that she might appease the gods who so drowned the world in such a deluge.

"They think I've anything to do with this?" cried Miri in exasperation, as yet another soaked envoy left grumbling from the harried priestess' hall. The familiar smell of the altar's incense grew faint, overwhelmed by the heavy scent of petrichor that, like the rainwaters of its origin, flooded the stone hut.

"If not the gods, then who?" Diarmuid asked fairly from the altar place, where he leaned on the broom with which he was attempting to sweep floodwaters out.

"The fae folk, a sea serpent, the slow inevitable destruction of the Earth under mankind's ceaseless encroaching upon her sacred places..." Miri trailed off, wringing out her hair onto the floor. Diarmuid gave her a look of long suffering and sighed while sweeping the puddle out with the remaining floodwater.

"You know as well as I the fae haven't the power for this kind of magic. And we'd know if it were a monster. They always have some kind of demand, and so far we've encountered nothing but rain." He furrowed his brow in thought, leaning on the broom again. "Do you think it may be the giants?"

"Diarmuid, if you break my besom broom I'm going to be very upset," she replied in exasperation, but turned to sit upon the low bench and put a hand to her chin in thought. "It could be the giants. There's no telling what they get up to. You want to go find out?"

He didn't hear her; he was reverently placing the besom broom back above the altar place, looking excessively upset. "I didn't... Miri I'm so sorry-"

Her bark-like laughter cut him off mid-apology. "You look so serious! Diarmuid, it's just a tool, like any other. There's nothing sacred about it. You can use it to scurry rats from the larder for all I care. Anyways, about those giants. You may actually be on to something. Will you go to the Dorragh, and seek them there?"

He pondered for a moment. His reply was unexpected.

"Will you come with me?"

"Will I... Diarmuid, what?"

"You heard me. Come with me. If you don't, the villagers will just keep wearing out their welcome asking you to solve their problems, and I'm afraid," he cast a sideways glance at the stone barricade he'd built at the threshold, through which water still streamed determinedly, "if you stay here, I'll come back and you'll have washed away. Come with me," he reiterated excitedly. "To the Dorragh, the land of the giants. You'll know better how to deal with them than I."

She put a hand to her breast, casting a timid, though thoughtful glance at her surroundings, as though not quite sure how to feel about leaving them so abruptly. "Well I'm... I'm flattered you'd want me to accompany you. And I suppose... yes, you're right. I should go."

His face broke out into a bright and beaming smile. "Let us go then!"

"What- now?"

"Yes! If not now, when?"

She smiled her mischievous smile, bringing out the wrinkle at the bridge of her nose. The joy in his voice was infectious. "You win. Let me grab my cloak."

The rain had slowed as the sun began its descent but Miri still huddled deep within the folds of her yellow homespun mantle. Diarmuid, in contrast, smiled as the mist streamed down his face and soaked the threadbare linen tunic he wore beneath his leather armor.

"We've a bit of sailing to do," he said, as he pulled a coracle from the rushes along the banks of the burn.

She stared at him in horror. "You mean to pole me along these rapids in a coracle? Are you mad?"

"You'll only get a little wet, Miri," he wheedled. "I promise I won't overturn us."

"Lying is a sin in the eyes of the Lady, Diarmuid."

"Alright. I promise to do my best not to overturn us."

He stuck to his word... as well as he could. Luckily they both could swim.

"By the gods... how is there so much water everywhere?" Miri groaned faintly as the burn began to flow amidst a delta of other, newer springs that lead into the massive and magnificent Lough Neagh; the large and legendary lake that lay like a sapphire jewel in the center of Eire. He poled them away from the rapid currents and switched to oars as they entered the open waters of the lake. Here the rain had softened almost entirely, turning instead to a white and eerie mist. Before them, on the opposite bank, loomed the mighty hills of the Dorragh - the land of the giants.

"Hmm. They aren't as big as I remember them," Miri said under her breath.

"You've been to the Dorragh?" He turned to regard her with a look of wonder. "But I thought the ancient King of Eire promised the giants no man would set foot in their lands for at least..."

"A hundred years. Yes, I know. I was there."

The mist seemed to thicken, and the rhythmic sound of the oars hitting the water slowed.

"Diarmuid. You asked me once how old I was, and I refused to tell you. I appreciate you never having asked me again. The truth is," she inhaled sharply, and clutched the folds of her dress with white knuckles, "I can't tell you. I don't actually know. I lost count over a dozen or so years ago, long after I had seen a century rise and fall. The wise woman who came before me, the one who claimed me as apprentice and saved my life when I so foolishly tried to end it, she lived even longer than I have done. I can only imagine her own predecessor descended from the fae folk, or even the gods themselves. I do not know," she said, turning a fathomless expression on him, "why we are so long lived, why we are made to watch the rise and fall of an entire era before we are let to join the ones we once loved in the kingdom of Tir na nOg."

"Is that why you've not taken an apprentice, then?" He asked quietly. "You do not wish to pass this on to anyone else?"

She tensed, and he began to think he may have crossed a line. "I'm sorry. Forget what I said. I... appreciate your honesty, and for what it's worth, I can only be thankful you've lived so long, that I might benefit from your wisdom."

"Oh, that's so, isn't it?" She frowned, but he could see the smile dancing in her eyes. "That's news to me. I never thought anything I've told you made it through that thick skull of yours."

He laughed, the sound echoing faintly in the deepening fog. "We must be nearly there," he insisted, as he gauged the darkness of the water below, thinking he could see the rocky shallows as they rowed beyond its greatest depths. And sure enough, though they could barely see the shore before the bottom of the coracle scraped it, they reached the far bank from which the misty heights of the Dorragh could be seen.

They disembarked upon the pebbly beach, and Diarmuid

pulled the coracle further up the bank to prevent it from washing away. Miri hastened to catch up to him, blocking him from stepping off the shore and onto the grassy slopes of the hill.

"Careful, Diarmuid. There's a special path meant only for the giants to see. If you stray from it, you'll wander aimlessly among these hills until the day the final horns sound and Eire sinks into the sea. If you would, stay closely behind me, please."

She seemed to feel around for a moment, then suddenly grasped at the empty air.

Empty, but for a fine golden thread she wove gently through her fingers.

"Aha. You won't be able to touch this, I'm afraid," she looked at him apologetically. "I'll have to guide you."

She stretched out her empty hand and he laced his fingers through hers. Her palms were warm again, and he thrilled to her touch.

"Now we need to find the gatekeeper. She must be close."

They set off at a steady pace, following the thread as it wound away from the beach and up to the grassy foothills. Even here water ran with abandon, flowing down the hills in rivulets and waterfalls of varying intensity and size. Some ran into flatlands, flooding into marshy ponds. Beside one of these they spotted a woman, crouching knee deep in its waters with a net in her hand.

"Hail, gatekeeper!" Miri hollered, keeping one hand firmly on the thread and the other on Diarmuid. "Have we found the way to the Dorragh, where live the last of the giants of Eire?"

"Eh?" The woman turned. Diarmuid suddenly noticed she was farther off than he initially thought. She cupped a hand to her ear. A hand, Diarmuid realized, that could easily clutch his whole torso in its bony fingers. "Speak up then, lass. I hardly hear ye nought."

"Are you not Thorga, the giantess who guards the gate of the Dorragh?" Miri spoke slightly louder, wincing in apology at Diarmuid.

"Aye, that I am, child. And who be ye?"

"I am Qimmirea, priestess of the Morrigan and *bean feasa* to the gods who rule in the land of Eire. I travel with Diarmuid, a... blacksmith," she squeezed his hand and he quickly assumed a blank expression to wipe away his confused one.

"What business have ye with the Dorragh? We be not fond of men, nor gods neither, as you should well know, *bean feasa*," she frowned.

"This rain. We mean to find its source, for it drowns all of Eire and ceases not for any reason. Know you why it falls so incessantly?" Her tone was polite and deferential, though Diarmuid could sense she bristled at the giantess' disdain for the gods.

"Ah, that. Shoulda known it would mean we get bothered by ye little folk. But who am I to tell Aelfryth to dry her tears?" The giantess shrugged, as though this should explain the matter.

Clearly, it didn't. Miri and Diarmuid cast a look of confusion at one another, and Miri turned back to the giantess. "You mean... all this rain. It's a giantess... crying?"

"O' course it be. What else could it?" She sniggered, tugging the net through the murky marshes laconically. "Aelfryth hain't got over her man pitching her. And til he be got over, she will never stop crying about him. She were always soft like that, that Aelfryth. She got it from her da', most sensitive man I ever did meet."

Miri's fingers flexed as she stifled a long, irritated sigh. "Who is Aelfryth? And who's this, this... lover?"

"You mean ye've never heard the tale of Aelfryth and Ruan?"

Her look soured. "Is it anything like the tale of Lisette and Gunnar? Isolt and Tristram? Grainne and-"

Thorga cut her off with a wave of her hands. "Stop, stop! I can tell ye've no got the heart for romance. But the lad here," and she winked lasciviously at Diarmuid, who gulped, "is keen on the hearin' o' it."

Miri puffed, trying to clear a straggling lock of hair that stuck to her forehead, wet with the streaming rain that simply would not stop falling. She turned her indigo eyes on Diarmuid, who couldn't quite keep the eager expression out of his own.

"Go on then. Tell the lad the tale. I'll wait," she sighed, gesturing for the giantess to continue.

Her wrinkled face spread into a grin. "Aye, that's more like it then. Aelfryth were a beautiful lass; the most beautiful, some say, though she's nought compared to the comeliness of her mother," and Thorga fluttered her tangled lashes beseechingly at Diarmuid. Miri shook her head in disbelief. "T'any rate, she were at once beset upon by all the eligible lads in Dorragh. One day she were in love with one, and the next day 'twas another. Til Ruan came.

"Ruan was a handsome and strong lad, and he knelt at her feet, and he promised he should earn the right to call her his bride by feats of great valor and great glory. She liked that, Aelfryth did, for most o' the others seemed to think she were won by soft speeches and useless trinkets. So she agreed, saying that once he returned from his quest, they would wed. Oh, the tears she wept at his parting! The oaths she made that she'd never love another! 'Til word came from someone that Ruan had vanished on Eire, and married elsewhere, meaning never to return again to the Dorragh or his fair Aelfryth. And the tears she wept then were nothing compared to the tears she weeps now. I do feel sorry for the child, I do," and she wiped her sunken, soft brown eyes, "but tain't like he were the only one of the Dorragh who sought her hand."

"So, let me guess," Miri's voice was light, but she cast a look of resignation at Diarmuid, "there's no stopping this rain till we find the rights of this Ruan fellow? The truth of whether he really abandoned Aelfryth to marry someone else, or if he was swallowed in a pit of his own hubris?"

"His own what now?" The giantess repeated perplexedly.

"Never mind. Do you think Aelfryth believes he might still be loyal to her?"

"Aye, that be true, for if she'd really given up hope, she'd no more be so upset as she is," nodded Thorga.

"Then it looks like," Miri tossed her eyes to the heavens, still keeping her hands gripped firmly on the thread and Diarmuid, though he could tell with every fiber of her being did she want to throw them up in disgust, "we have to go hunt down a wandering hero. Did he mention any feat of wonder in particular?"

"Well, he said summat about a treasure lying untouched in a castle surrounded by a ring o' everlasting fire..."

"Gods preserve me. Of course he did. Come on, Diarmuid," and she tugged the warrior back along the path, "and thank you most kindly, noble Thorga."

Diarmuid waited until they'd marched all the way down the path, back to the coracle that floated patiently on the rocky beach, and he waited until she let go of the golden thread and his hand and clutched her face, unleashing a violent and guttural groan of utter defeat. "GIANTS! I swear on the Lady, they've not changed a bit."

"Well. At least we know where the rain comes from?" He offered with a shrug.

Narrowing her eyes, she simply lifted the hood of her mantle and disappeared within it, cursing under her breath at the ceaseless deluge.

They made their way to a cave alongside Lough Neagh, pulling the coracle behind them in order to keep it from drifting off during the night. Diarmuid built a smoky little fire, using the thankfully dry tinder some thoughtful prior traveler had left behind.

"I thank you again priestess, for your company," he insisted, as they both drank from the ever full jug she wore at her hip. "I know these aren't the... best of conditions. But the road does grow lonely after a while."

"I thought you were past master at the art of the lonely wandering hero," she quizzed him lethargically. She was staring into the fire, but then shook herself from her reverie. "I'm not averse to the adventure. I just don't want to get in your way."

He made to speak, but she silenced him. "I don't need your empty platitudes, hero," she said with her crooked smile. "Just let me tell it like it is, sometimes."

Hurt, but unwilling to refute her, he turned his own face to the fire, and watched as it dwindled to embers. But suddenly she slid a hand over his and squeezed his fingers lightly, though her eyes were still downcast.

"I'm sorry. That wasn't very kind of me."

"You really think I need you so little?" He responded, and her heart jumped to her throat at the sight of the sincerity and conflict in his eyes.

"I... well. I don't expect you to need me. I rather expect you to be tired of me, if I'm honest, as I am rather annoyingly officious sometimes and probably unbearably overbearing and–"

He cups her jaw in his hand, stroking it softly with his thumb, turning her face to look at his. Her lips part softly as she goes mute. He feels her damp breath on his mouth as he leans forward to taste of the honey on her tongue, to drown his thirst in her forgiving embrace.

He ran out of words. He has none, really, that can explain the fire in his veins when he holds her. The peace and clarity of mind that he finds only in her presence. The force of his desire, the strength of his yearning, to tell her all the things he's locked away for so long burst forth in a flood and before he is washed away entirely he looks at her, and she at him, and suddenly, they know in a moment that words wouldn't be enough.

She nearly tears through his threadbare tunic. He winds his fingers in her hair and presses her body so hard with his that she gasps, winded by his ardour. Her dress is pushed up around her waist as he grabs her hips to meet his tongue. He buries his face between her legs, tasting her fiery nectar and feeling her thighs flex and contract as she moans and shivers in pleasure. When he finally looks up at her, she's crying, and he can do nothing but hold her close and feel her tears mingle with his own.

There are many tales of the *bean feasa*; the seeresses bidden by the gods to speak prophecies of great heroes, who will triumph and fall to mighty deeds on behalf of the greatness of mankind. It is strange so few of these stories seem to feature the love between such characters. For what is a hero without a priestess to foretell his future? What good is a seer if the object of her sight never manifests?

But here, in a tiny smoky cave tucked away below the Dorragh, on the rocky banks of Lough Neagh, the love of two such beings is consecrated. They do not speak of it. They do not give it a name; a face; a purpose. It is enough that they are simply together in this moment, whispering their desire to one another, pledging faith with bodies that meet and meet again in passionate, mystical ecstasy. Some things simply go without saying.

Every story has an end, and they don't know when theirs will be. They hold to each other with urgency, desire, passion - born from the simple truth that tomorrow they may die. But today, they live.

The embers dwindle into ash.

—

The day shone clearer than it had in a long time. Fits of rain still persisted, but every now and again patchy sunlight burst determinedly through the blanket of clouds. They again poled the coracle out over the open lake before switching to oars once they reached its depths. Out in the center of the lake stood a smattering of islands that rose from the open water. Some bore cairns of boulders and craggy rocks, others soft grassy mounds upon which golden sheep grazed, tended by keen eyed giants who stood menacingly at the banks as though daring the boat to try and beach. However, Diarmuid knew his course and drifted not from it. For he too knew of the tale of the legendary castle around which an eternal fire burned, and kept the prow of the coracle pointed toward the mystical isle upon which it stood.

They drew up on the gravelly beach and again dragged the coracle clear of the water's reach. Very easily could they tell they came to the right place. A great wall of fire burned before them, rising ever higher in the sky. Diarmuid squinted upwards but even he couldn't see where the flames ended and the sky began.

"How do we even begin to breach this?" He turned toward Miri, clearly perplexed.

"The last hero kind of just, rode through. On a horse."

"A horse? Was he mad? How is such a thing even possible?"

She shrugged, with that telltale wrinkle on the bridge of her nose. "It must've been a fast horse."

He snorted and crossed his arms, regarding the fire with a raised eyebrow. "Well, we've not got one of those, fast or otherwise. Did the hero wear any special armor?"

"What, other than plot armor?" She quipped with her playful grin. "It's a story, Diarmuid. A fable, meant to teach us something too subtle to learn of our own accord."

The blaze brightened every so often, fed by gusts of wind. The rain affected it not, drops merely hissing and evaporating once within range of the fire's oppressive heat.

He knew the story she referred to, of course. The ancient tale of Siegurd and Brunille, the warrior who vanquished the legendary Fafnir and then entered the castle surrounded by Odin's eternal fire to seek the sleeping maiden, once a mighty Valkryie, who lay within.

Just another hopeless challenge, he thought with chagrin. *Another deed that calls for me to conquer it though I've no guidance or direction but my own.*

But two heroes have managed to part this blazing curtain. And I shall be the third.

"Miri," he said suddenly. "Do you think me the greatest and most powerful warrior in all of Eire?"

"I don't even think you're the greatest or most powerful warrior on this isla- oh. Oh I see what you're doing. Don't even try it, Diarmuid," she replied warningly.

"Come on now, just give me this one," he wheedled. "You know better than I that the Morrigan has yet to call for me."

"This isn't the Morrigan's fire, Diarmuid, it's Odin's," she argued.

"But this isn't Odin's land. It's the Tuatha de Danann's. This will work, I know it will."

She sighed, and he thought in the depths of her eyes he could actually see a true, moving pride; a look he'd often caught when she spoke of Hrothgir or the other great kings of old. That look stirred in his breast and he felt a lightness spread through every inch of him, raising the hairs on his flesh and tingling all over.

"I, Qimmirea, priestess of the Morrigan," she said calmly, and with a conviction he felt to his core, "do believe you, Diarmuid, to be the greatest and the strongest warrior of all Eire."

He grinned. And without a backward glance, he walked through the towering pillar of eternal fire.

—

Inside the space was hushed, almost supernaturally quiet. Though he knew it rained, the drops fell with nary a whisper. He approached the high wooden doors of the castle and pushed them. Though they were heavy, and cumbersome, they opened without a creak. His footsteps on the flagstones were muffled and yet still the warrior strained for any sound, or noise, always wary of danger.

But none came. He could see through the yawning portals

in the stone castle walls heaps of gold, massive piles of treasures, and weapons that surpassed any he'd seen or made before. These trifles distracted him not. He knew that the one he sought lay somewhere deeper within the castle, and he knew too this ancient treasure bore a deep and miserable curse.

Finally, he came upon a throne room stacked high with ingots of gold and silver, furnished with cloth of silk and gold, and paved with stone and gems that glittered in the dim light filtering through high stained glass windows. Upon the tall throne sat a man. And that man, Diarmuid could tell in a moment, was as wide as Diarmuid was tall and when standing would reach the height of three men standing on one another's shoulders.

He was also fast asleep.

"Don't tell me... you attempted..." Diarmuid whispered to himself, staring at the breastplate fixed awkwardly across the giant's massive torso.

To be fair, the breastplate was magnificent. A thing of wondrous beauty, and clearly great power and strength; crafted by Odin himself to protect the Valkyrie who originally bore it. But of course it ill fitted this massive giant. Diarmuid simply sighed and shook his head at the greed that caused Ruan to forget about the thorn of sleep embedded in its metal plates before trying to don it.

"Aelfryth... your future husband may be a brave warrior, but he's definitely not the smartest one," he muttered. Stretching out his spear, he sliced the leather straps that buckled the breastplate to the sleeping giant and it clattered to the floor.

"SK- wha? Who? Who are you? Do you dare to steal my

treasure; slay me in my sleep like a coward!" boomed the giant Ruan as he stumbled sleepily to his feet.

"If I wanted to slay you in your sleep you'd be dead," assured Diarmuid, with a deadly glitter in his fearless blue eyes that even the giant recognized. "But I don't. I just want you to go home to your Aelfryth, so she'll stop crying and flooding all of Eire."

"Aelfryth? My Aelfryth! My soft, tender beauty! She weeps for her lost love! Aye, I will go to her, I will go to her this minute! But first," he looked around, and reached for the breastplate, "my armor, that is, my treasure-"

Diarmuid, again with the end of his spear, smacked the breastplate from the giant's hand. "You fool. Odin placed within that breastplate the thorn of sleep, so it would protect the Valkyrie Brunille until the greatest and the strongest warrior in the land came to rescue her. Haven't you heard the tale?" He asked sternly.

The giant looked sheepish. "Yes, well, but I didn't think it were true."

"It is. And that's why you've been stuck here. Do not repeat your mistakes. Just go, and return to Aelfryth, and please," Diarmuid insisted, and though his tone was polite again that deadly glitter shone in his eyes, "neither return to Eire, nor seek lost treasures guarded by ancient gods."

"Fine. Were it not for you, I would slumber here til Ragnarok. So I suppose I will do as you say. Farewell, good hero." And just like that the giant took leave of the castle, parting the curtain of fire as though it were made of naught but silk.

"That kind of confidence..." Diarmuid shook his head incredulously. With a helpless shrug he too left the castle, and passed through the fire that burned eternally into an endless sky.

—

"And he almost put the breastplate back on? Diarmuid, you must be joking."

"I wish I were," groaned the warrior with a smile, reclining in the sun on one of the gravestones in the yard before the oratory. "But as ever, I am deadly serious."

The boisterous breezes of summer skirted along the horizon, and a crisp brightness settled on the leaves that unfurled on erstwhile naked trees. Miri breathed deep, the air clear now that the ceaseless tears of Aelfryth had dried, and she smiled.

Giants, indeed.

X

WHERE TREAD THE

OLD GODS

She walks quietly, with purpose; bare feet padding along the roughly hewn planks of the dock. A smile creeps its way into the corners of her mouth as she sees the puddles of melted wax dripping from still-lit tapers that marked the pathway.

I'll give him points for trying, she thinks to herself with a roll of the eyes. *At least it's not rose petals.*

She shouldn't have held her breath. Reaching the boat that rocked gently on the water she could see, even in the dim candlelight, the telltale sign of flower petals littering the deck. As she cautiously stepped aboard those petals began to mark a distinct pathway toward a pelt bundled rather unceremoniously between two benches. She had to bite her lip to keep from laughing outright, in case he were in earshot.

He didn't have to try quite so hard. And he better put that back, that's my best lambskin.

Settling herself gingerly amidst the pile of soft fur and straw stuffed pillows, she smiled graciously at the moonlight upon her face. She breathed deeply of the spicy tang of clover that had been baking all day in the summer sun and had since opened its dewy hearts and vibrant fragrance to the evening air.

Yes, she thought, *perhaps I could get used to this. Maybe I shouldn't have turned down so many offerings as I had-*

She feels hands slide from her shoulders down to her waist, and arms draw her into a chest both firm, and bare.

"Still clothed," he whispered into her ear, his teeth grazing the bottom of her lobe and sending shivers from the crown of her head to the tips of her toes. "I would've thought you'd get the hint."

She leaned back into the comforting circle of his arms, for once not even pretending to take umbrage at his cheek. "I figured you'd prefer to do the honors."

"Oh priestess," he breathed, his hands now under her kirtle and bundling it swiftly over her head, "that isn't even the least of the liberties I plan to take with you."

He was in earnest. She bent herself over the bench, presenting him with a moon as full as the one above, arching slightly as she felt his fingers slide between her thighs.

The ritual begins, she thinks to herself, even as she knows the goddess filled little space between them this night.

His tongue met her flesh, the cleft between her cheeks. She shivered and felt a blush begin to creep its way across her face; not at the intimacy with which he devoured her but at the desperation with which his body explored hers. And then she hadn't even room to think of that as the urgency with which he massaged her both with his mouth and his hands increased. Her actual knees began to feel weak, and she thanked every star she could see for how conveniently boats were designed for such activities from her comfortable perch on the bench.

"A whisper to the sky, but not to me," he pouted mockingly as he momentarily came up for air.

"You'll get your blessings soon enough," she replied somewhat breathlessly, almost laughing at the weakness in her voice that matched the jelly of her legs. "Make it worth it first."

He wiped his mouth with an almost savage grin, leaning forward to press his lips against her shoulder, her collar, her neck. She sighed almost involuntarily, body unconsciously striving towards his as his sharp teeth dragged along her skin.

He finds it so easy to mount her. To slip inside her with the ease which his sword slips into its sheath - an apt comparison, he thinks to himself, as he grabs her hips to bury himself deeper in her and bends his neck to bury his face deeper into her hair. In her throat he hears the rasp of a moan she refuses to exhale, and with an unseen smirk he twists his hips and runs a thumb along the slick softness parting between her legs.

The rasp turns into a cry. His name, her voice, carried across the water in that little bay.

He will make that cry worth it. He wants her, by all the gods does he want her. And he knows as she sighs and bucks beneath him that she wants him too. Her body is soft, but not fragile; he can grab her with the strength of his hands as they were worked by the forge and feel her bend not like brittle wood but like heated iron, giving but little under each measured stroke.

So he strikes harder. And harder still. Their flesh meets with a sound almost as loud as the hammer hitting the anvil. But she wraps her arms around him and twists her fingers in his hair and meets him stroke for stroke.

I cannot bend you, priestess, he thinks to himself with a hand to her throat and his thumb pressed against her bottom lip. *You are as strong and unyielding as the gods ever made you.*

Perhaps she can see this in the depths of his eyes. It is not inadequacy, but the frustration of facing an unattainable and unbreachable barrier. With every stroke she feels closer to him and so with every measured stroke she draws herself further away. *It's just sex, Miri,* she tells herself. *It means nothing to me, and less to him; it is meant only as an offering to the goddess.*

Both she and the goddess know she is lying.

Suddenly she stops, pressing a hand to Diarmuid's chest. He looks at her quizzically, almost hurt, but withdraws from her instantly.

"Lay down," she says, her commanding tone somehow fragile in spite of her best efforts. He senses this and obeys her, overcoming the rising insecurity and realizing, with sudden clarity, what she needs him to do.

"Miri," he whispers, reclining against the furs, the moonlight reflecting warmth in the depths of those icy blue eyes.

He says only her name. But she straddles him, and slips him inside her, and suddenly the rest of the speech is clear as day.

It is not ritual, and it is not passionless. Not by any stretch. As she sways her hips against his, matching the rhythm of his arcing pelvis with her own, she actually sighs in pleasure. True, pure, uncomplicated pleasure.

She leans forward for better purchase, still matching every thrust with one of her own. He puts a hand forth to stroke the hair from her face, running his thumb along her cheek and over her lower lip. She takes it between her teeth and sucks, almost cooing in pleasure as he gently grips her face.

He, too, exhales in delight, short breaths of growing intimacy and desire that match the look on his face. She feels him flex and convulse beneath her, drawn almost to the edge by the rocking of her hips, and she slows, gently pulling his hand from her mouth.

"I am not done with you yet, warrior," she hisses playfully.

"Good," he replies, sitting up to grab her waist and thrust deeper inside of her, bending her backwards over the bench and kissing the space between her breasts. "I'm not done with you either."

Their breathy moans and longing sighs soon turned to shouts, to shrieks, to laughs. He pulls her hair to throw her head back and expose her throat to his teeth, leaving blooming roses in a line along her skin. She is so tangled in him that she can feel his heartbeat through his skin, and hers. The heat of his blood flowing as it did in his veins, between his legs, between hers. In the depths of a passion she has never felt before she cries out again, to the goddess, to him.

To herself, a promise and an apology, for the fetters
with which she bound herself before. As she is now
completely, utterly, and irreversibly unbound by him.

"I want you," she swallows, the words almost inaudible,
"to finish inside me, to finish with me. I am so close, and
yet..." She clings almost unconsciously to him, almost
admitting that she did not want to let him go.

He responds by embracing her tighter. Burying his face
in her hair, at her neck. Feeling the softness of her skin
against his, the softness of her sentiment like an unguent
that soothes his fevered soul.

He loves her. And finally she believes it. They lock eyes
in the heat of their shared moment before closing them
slowly, succumbing to its power. Waves of pleasure roll
through both of them, matched in the physical responses
of their bodies and the spiritual responses of their hearts.

She snuggles up to him, both breathing heavily, and he
wraps an arm around her shoulders and draws her close.
The moon has set, leaving only stars sparkling in the skies
above and on the still waters. For a moment she feels
suspended, as though floating weightlessly in that great
expanse beyond the sky that arcs over Eire. Between here,
and the further glorious home of the gods. It is a place she
has long been familiar with.

And yet for the first time, she realizes, as he presses a kiss
to the crown of her head and whispers words of love in
her ear, she is not alone.

—

She'd forgone her embroidered kirtle and woolen apron
in favor of a soft tunic of woven cloth lined with rabbit's

fur, and her bare legs for leather breeches. A leather thong bound her hair back from her freckled forehead. He was surprised to see how bright and youthful her eyes shone when not shaded by her coils of fiery hair.

"I'm glad you chose to answer the king's call," Diarmuid said appreciatively, as they both loaded onto one of the longboats docked on the banks of the Fyroe.

"Never will you catch me missing a journey like this. To brave the open seas in search of that which has never been seen before; to follow the paths of the gods themselves! No mortal man has set foot where we are about to tread for a thousand years or more," Qimmirea replied eagerly, eyes alight in anticipation of adventure.

That particular point had posed something of a problem when it came to encouraging the might of Bjirtka's finest to set off on such a voyage. The hardy folk of Eire's coastal village spoiled for war, for feats of daring and of strength. Though perhaps they may face a legendary sea serpent or other monster of the deep, they regretted the lack of call to arms. And what good were rocks and floes of ice if neither gold nor riches lay among them?

But King Hrothgir knew how to be persuasive and turn the minds of men who longed for war to brighter vistas. They sought the old homes of the ancient gods, the mighty and fabled land of Cait Neth. Who knew really what treasure may lay there? Or what feats of wonder and magic they may discover?

The sight of the fleet that lay in the bright waters of the Fyroe stirred even the most hardened of their crew's hearts. Bright red sailcloth rippled in a fine, late summer breeze. The low rolling of drums that measured the strokes the oarsmen would take echoed throughout the valley. Though they sailed not for war, or glory in battle, they knew their voyage would become one of the oldest sagas and their names carry on the lips of their people for generations to come.

The old warriors hailed Miri as she boarded and clapped Diarmuid upon his broad back. Ever were they favorites of Bjirtka's men and women. Especially among these, who possessed the souls of the old ways and hearts belonging to the traditions of the gods.

Miri seated herself beside Diarmuid at the handle of a long oar that jutted from the side of the boat. As the drum's tempo slowly increased they pulled along with the crew, heading along the trail of bright sunlight reflecting upon the water toward the open sea.

"What seek you then, good priestess?" Diarmuid asked when the sails began to fill and their tempo slowed, becoming casual enough for speech.

"Hmm? On Cait Neth, you mean?" she asked. Her eyes were bright, the colour of the sea as the sun set beyond it.

"Sure; on Cait Neth, or even here, on the ocean."

"Why, here I get to be among my people." She smiled, nodding with a grin at the oarsmen around her, pulling their own way with looks of determination on their faces. "Life always moves on in Eire. New kings mount old thrones, villages die and are reborn again. It's hard to keep up. But here," she paused, as a flock of baying gulls soared overhead, "time means nothing. It is naught but the sea, and the strength of man against it. Cait Neth is a crown jewel of our history. There lie the gods, the old ways, that gave us spirit and taught us life. I would see with my own eyes the truth of the fables around which we revolve, and," she sighed faintly, "bring back memories of those tales, to remind those who come after us of the glories that came before."

Night fell quickly. They watched the aurora burn brightly overhead; could hear it crackle and hum, glowing with the fires of the gods' chariots as they rode through the sky. It fluttered like a floating banner held aloft by rippling winds in shifting shades of green and white, flaring occasionally into the pinks and creams of an ocean sunrise, against the flawless sapphire night sky. A lone sailor began to sing, her voice carrying among the boats a lilting corsair tune that filled the hearts and throats of all aboard the longships that floated on the sea. As the night grew deeper they tied the boats off to one another and the sailors settled close together into the spaces between the benches for warmth, for the further north they went the colder the air around them became.

"And you, Diarmuid?" whispered Miri from his shoulder where she lay wide awake, watching the torchlight held by the sentries flicker in his eyes. "What do you hope to find on Cait Neth?"

"The seat of the Morrigan, that I may bow before it and offer myself up to her as humble tribute."

"Be serious, or I'll roll over and go to sleep."

He chuckled. "You know me too well." He stroked her hair absently, while trying to answer her question honestly. "I don't know if I seek any one thing in particular. When King Hrothgir's missive reached us, all I could think about was the adventure. The sight of blue waves stretched as far as the eye can see, the mystical island that rises from the cold waters, the very feat of facing the open ocean with naught but my strength." *And you.*

She sat up to look at him, and he shifted guiltily, wondering if she could read his thoughts. *My thoughts that never once strayed from the Morrigan. They wander like a flock without its shepherd, of late.*

"I hope you find it, then," was all she said, settling back down against him with a quiet sigh. "That which you do not know you are looking for."

He opened his mouth but closed it, unsure how to address the double meaning in her words. With another quiet laugh, he simply wrapped her closer and closed his eyes, drifting off to sleep with the mighty aurora burning overhead.

Morning brought a welcome sight. Surrounding the boats and swimming below them teemed schools of silver fish, their dappled scales dancing with light. The warriors began to point and gabble excitedly, throwing hand lines and nets out into the water to draw the promised feast aboard.

The sea grew quiet but for the joyous cries of the fishing men who heaped the bounty upon the boats. Miri studied the water closely, and suddenly the blood drained from her face.

"Pull!" she screamed with all her might, that every boat may hear her. "Row, for your lives and the lives of your unborn children!"

They heard her, and the eldest amongst the boats dropped their lines without hesitation and rowed with all their strength. The younger looked on in confusion, not willing to lose the bounteous school.

That is, until they saw in the rippling depths the sea bottom rise to meet them and the waters begin to froth and churn, capsizing their boats and flinging them into the waiting maw of a great sea monster.

Four boats were lost in this way. Of those boats, few survivors were pulled from the churning waters before they too could meet the fate of their brethren. The warriors shouted frantically, flinging arrows and spears into the hide of the great beast, turning the seas red with its blood. It writhed frantically, washing the boats closest to it with waves of sea water, that they had to bail with all haste before they, too, could sink into the ocean.

Suddenly they heard a cry. A warrior, poised on the prow of one of the closest ships, hefted a massive spear carved with the undulating lines of a snake over his shoulder. The boat rocked from the force of one wave, then two, and then the warrior released his spear, aiming it for the creature's roving, bloodshot eye.

The shot told. It gave a final spasm, sank into the murky waters, and then slowly bobbed to the surface, its slick hide glistening with blood and seawater.

"Kivan! What a mighty throw!" whooped Miri, as she recognized the warrior who stood upon the prow of the ship.

Others took up her cry, hailing the warrior with praise for their salvation. He nodded deeply, mouth set in a thin grim line, then leaned out over the corpse of the sea monster to retrieve his spear and wash it clean of the monster's viscera and blood in the salty waves.

As the surface of the water settled they poled slowly

among the wreckage of the lost longships in the vain hope
they might rescue any survivors. But once the sun hit its
zenith the sentries aboard each ship wound their horns,
and once again the rhythmic drums began to pound.
They could waste no more time, and with heavy hearts
they settled back to the benches and rowed for Cait Neth.

"What manner of beast was that, Miri?" Diarmuid asked,
when the silence grew too great to be born.

She shook herself, thinking deeply. "Have you heard of
the three hearts of Meiche?"

He nodded. The fabled son of the Morrigan was a famous
figure. "You refer to the tale that his hearts contained
serpents, then?"

She rowed in silence for a moment. Then she spoke, her
voice matching the cadence of the drums and carrying to
the ears of all aboard the kenning and even to those who
rowed in the boats beside them.

"In an arch above the Fyroe, over the waterfall from
which it springs high up in the highest mountains of Eire,
there lies an inscription. Its words are old, the tongue
in which it is written even older. But there, carved into
that arch of stone, is the tale of Meiche. The son of the
Morrigan, in whose chest beat three hearts, one for each
of her forms.

"A hero," she smiled mysteriously, "sought to defeat
Meiche, for it was told he would bring the end to Eire and
wash it in a flood of its people's blood. He knew of the
three hearts; he knew a strike to a single heart would not
be enough to defeat him. But Meiche was protected by
the divine strength of his mother, and it was foretold that
only one strike could bring his end.

"So the hero climbed the waterfall, to the high tops of the highest mountains in Eire. Meiche saw the hero's approach and did nothing. For he knew that he would fall to only a single strike, and that one strike could not stop all three of the hearts within him.

"But the hero was cunning. He bore a massive spear carved in the likeness of a snake, and as he reached the top of the waterfall he commanded Meiche to appear and face him. Meiche did, crossing his arms over his chest and jeering at the bold warrior.

"'I bid you, Meiche, son of the Morrigan,' cried the hero, 'To look your last upon the setting sun. Praise the sky above you while you can, for today will be the end, and I will slay you in a single strike, that you may not live to bring the end to Eire and drown its people in a flood of their own blood. I give you this moment, and this one only,' he said firmly, 'To make your peace with the gods above before you go to meet them.'

"Meiche, though he laughed at the warrior's daring, decided to do as the warrior bid. For what mattered it? He would praise the gods that so graced him with three hearts - he would ask their bounty, that he may slay this warrior who dared to challenge him. He turned to face the setting sun, he raised his arms above his head, in calling upon the Tuatha de Danann and his own divine mother.

"As he raised his arms, so too did the hero raise his spear, and the eyes of the snake engraved along its shaft seemed to glitter. With a single, mighty throw he pitched the spear into Meiche's side - the strength of his thrust entering the mighty being's first heart, then the second, then the third. Meiche collapsed, stricken, with a single blow that had at once pierced all three of his hearts.

"'A curse upon you, hero!' he cried as he lay dying. 'And a curse on this land, that I may no longer walk upon! You have pierced my hearts - and from each of them, as they beat their last, a serpent will spring. One to swim in the lakes, and one to flow in the rivers, and one to dive the mighty depths of the sea. I will not be the end of Eire, I will not live to see my destiny through. But these serpents will plague you, and your sons, and your sons' sons,' he swore, 'and never shall you live in peace, until they grow large enough to swallow this land whole!'

"And with a last, ragged breath, he died. The hero brought his spear to bear, hoping to slay the serpents before they escaped, but he moved too slowly. They slithered quickly out of sight, one to the lakes, one to the rivers, and one to the depths of the sea. The hero strove long and sought for them until the day he last drew breath, but none could he find, nor his sons, nor his sons' sons, though they all took up the mantle of their father before them and hunted the serpents that sprang from the hearts of the slain Meiche. And it is not until this day," she said finally, with a long look at Kivan- the son of Fergus, who was the son of Finn, who was, or so the legends told, the son of Mac Cecht, the great hero who had slain Meiche with a single thrust of his spear- "that any have ever faced one."

Diarmuid bowed his head in thanks for her tale, and the oarsmen all followed suit. She smiled graciously, the light of her spirit that loved speaking in the old tongue still bright upon her face.

Though they mourned the loss of their comrades, they all knew the dangers of this voyage and so could not long suppress the joy that swelled within them at the sight of land off into the distance. For before them lay Cait Neth, the jewel of the open sea, the seat of the old gods.

The boats entered a harbor, one into which a river flowed. They dropped their sails, rowing rhythmically up the river mouth, staring in wide-eyed wonder at the scenery surrounding them. Ice, glaciers that seemed to climb for leagues and leagues into the heavens themselves, rose up from the banks. Misty waterfalls cast rainbow light as the spray caught the glow of the setting sun. Despite the chill, hardy twisted trees and clinging moss grew from the rock that peeked occasionally from the walls of ice, and high up on the flat cliff tops they spotted grassy slopes upon which grey fox and mountain goat gave chase.

The pounding drums that measured the oarsmen's pulls echoed hauntingly, an ethereal music augmented by Miri's low pagan chanting. Some of the older warriors, in whose mouths the old tongue lived still, chanted with her.

They knew the might of nature would ever outweigh the wit of man.

At last they came to a cave that yawned into the cliff side. Upon it were runes carved into the stone, still slightly visible though nearly completely effaced by the water and ice that eroded the cave's walls. As they entered the cave the blackness swallowed up the light from their torches, and the silence remained complete but for the soft splash of the oars slowly pulling through the still waters.

They disembarked at a large bank of flat rock that led up to a clearing rising above the water's edge. A massive hole punctured the cave's ceiling overhead through which shone the dying light of the sun. They made camp quickly, building tents from the hides and blankets upon which they had slept in the boats and stringing the fish up to dry between them. Several warriors formed a scouting party and set off to find a passage from the cave to the rest of the island beyond. Miri and, to her surprise, Diarmuid, remained behind.

"There is plenty here for me to do," he answered with a shrug in response to her inquisitive gaze. "I need not be the first to walk upon this land that has for so long lain untouched."

She admired his deference and recognized in it a feeling akin to her own. While she, too, longed to explore these untouched reaches, she knew that nowhere could men stand for long without leaving behind some of the destruction that seemed to follow wherever they go. With that in mind, as they all gathered that evening to plan the excursion on the morrow, she stood and addressed them all as their respected high priestess, from whose mouth the words of gods were spoken.

"You cannot shed blood in this sacred place, do you understand me? This land belongs to the old gods. One day they will die and there will be nothing left to stop us from seizing every corner of the Earth for our own means. But until that cursed day," she hissed in a low tone, a forbidding expression twisting her brow, "and so long as I draw breath, this place will belong to them, and not to us. Do not fight amongst yourselves - not for treasure, or for pleasure, or for boredom, or for spite. The bodies buried here will never cross to Tir na nOg," and each of the warriors looked grim at her speech, "and the hands from which that blood was spilled will be cursed for generations to come."

They promised, and at first their word was easily kept. The land proved more bountiful than ever they'd

imagined. Chests dug from the earth were filled with all
manner of dazzling gems, and fine metals, and weapons
whose balance and heft spoke them to be of legendary
might. Each night the boats grew heavier with the weight
of these spoils. And each day they ventured further, their
hearts full. For they had seen the mark of the gods on
this land and often fell to their knees in devout prayer at
feeling the brush of divinity against their mortal souls.

But perfect peace cannot last, even among the most
generous of folk. It was on this, the final night of their
exploration, that they were recalled to the spite, and
the jealousy, and the weakness that make men mortal.
Women vied for the treasures that their companions
culled. Men, whose weapons lay heavy in hands unused
to peace, grunted and spat their distaste for the idle
waste that lay upon these untouched lands. They thought
perhaps they should not go but instead stay; settle among
these fertile woods, and fell these immense trees, to build
homes in which they could sire children that would rule
in a land of their own and not in thrall of the kings and
queens of Eire whose rule and whose castles grew ever
less tenable in their wealth and splendor.

"We must leave at the first light of dawn," muttered
Miri under her breath to Diarmuid. She could sense the
growing ire in the hearts of the younger voyagers and
their desire to remain and claim this land for their own.
"If I were not worried about being too hasty, I would
demand we leave at once. I like this not, Diarmuid, and
neither do the gods."

He nodded in agreement, but knew not how to sway the
intention of their crew. He was, after all, an outsider, one
whose word carried no command to any of them. Out
of the corner of his eye he spotted Kivan staring into the
depths of the fire. He alone remained silent, his heart

seemingly untouched by the beauty of the isle nor the frenzy that stirred his companions. Forming an impulsive resolution, Diarmuid stood to greet the pensive warrior.

"Kivan," said Diarmuid, as he took a seat beside him. "you have influence among these people. Your might and your spear carry much weight. Should you be done here on the isle, perhaps you can convince them to leave this night. What is it you desire from Cait Neth?"

"I have found that which I seek," he replied, without turning to regard Diarmuid.

Diarmuid smiled in relief. But before he could speak, Kivan continued, the snapping of superheated sap in the heart of the fire matching the violence of the light in the warrior's eyes and the light of its flickering flames dancing on his restless brow.

"On this isle are traces of two serpents, the fiends born from the hearts of the slain Meiche. It is them, and only them, I hunt. And once I find them, I will slay them. And then the souls of my father, and my father's father, will finally be put to rest." He clenched the spear that had drawn the blood of the sea serpent with a powerful hand. The spear's glistening tip still bore traces of the creature's blood, dulling the deadly shine of its razor sharp edge.

Diarmuid swallowed hard, casting an uncomfortable glance at Miri. This was not how he'd expected the conversation to go. "You heard the priestess. The shedding of blood on this sacred land will unleash a woeful curse. Give up this mad quest, Kivan. The serpents are trapped here with the gods and can do the land of Eire no ill."

"I care not for the priestess. Nor the ire of the gods.

They cursed my family once already, and nothing can outweigh that curse."

"I cannot let you do this," began Diarmuid sorrowfully. Kivan scoffed, then suddenly shot to his feet, brandishing the serpentine spear with its bloodstained blade.

"On your own blood will you stop me, Diarmuid of Eillear. Though perhaps you are better known as Diarmuid, of nowhere in particular. What know you of sacred vows, and the aegis of ancestors for whom you raise your spear? What know you of children who live but for one single purpose, and to that purpose alone their life is sacrificed?"

Diarmuid winced, the weight of rage rising within him. He too clutched his spear, though he moved not toward the goading warrior.

"Diarmuid! Kivan! Stop this!" Miri shouted, stepping forward between them with her hands outstretched. "You know not the danger you court in this hallowed place!"

Kivan scoffed again. "Quiet, you ancient hag. I listen not to you, nor the vengeful and worthless gods for whom you claim to speak!" And he spat at her feet.

Then suddenly crashed to the stone floor, knocked off his own feet by a flying punch from Diarmuid.

"Say that again, you sniveling whelp, and the god's curse will be nothing compared to what I deliver unto you," he seethed, as the man struggled to rise.

But he was feinting. He launched himself at Diarmuid's knees, sending him sprawling onto the rocks just short of the water's edge. Their tussle was sharp and brutal, each landing blows on the other that would fell a steer. The rest of the crew watched in shock; mesmerized, and not willing to face the danger of attempting to sunder the two foes.

Finally, with an almighty splash, they toppled off the stony banks into the river itself. Diarmuid managed to wriggle free of his opponent's grip, and swam back for shore. He dove for his spear just as Kivan reached his own. They stood and drew their blades at one another's throats, panting heavily.

"Stop!" commanded Miri, before either could regain their senses enough to strike.

Suddenly they both felt rooted to the ground, unable to break the otherworldly force that gripped them. Above, in the skylight that opened in the ceiling of the cave the aurora flashed, bright forms and figures dancing across the night sky. A threnodic sough whispering of words in the old tongue seemed at once impossibly quiet and tremendously loud. A great raven, her wings glowing and scintillating, gave a hoarse cry, one that reverberated and echoed throughout the cave. A warrior upon her back, shrouded in a hooded cloak, swung a mace among the magnetic and ethereal clouds of light. He spoke imposingly in those incomprehensible words, and all the elders of the group dropped to their knees and touched their foreheads to the floor. Slowly, the others did the same, staring furtively at one another even as they felt the weight of the divine gods impress their importance upon their very souls.

Though the words were foreign, their import was clear. *You think you have forsaken us, you think this land is yours. You never can, and it never will be, for powers that transcend your own exist. They came before, and they will come after, long after you are gone.*

With a sound like a thunderclap the apparitions vanished. The two warriors stumbled as the magical grip released them. They looked long upon one another, violence and anger clear upon the face of each. Diarmuid straightened. And then, with a grimace, he dropped his spear.

"Slay me then, warrior. You say you do not honor the gods. But I do, and it is my soul that will join them in their hallowed halls. Slay me and take your bounty, do what you will. But you do so alone. Your fellow voyagers know the truth of this land now, and they will leave you here, never to return again."

Kivan saw the truth of what Diarmuid had said writ upon their faces. Though some, like him, had become skeptical of the might of the gods, they had all just seen the true nature of those they had so foolishly doubted. He threw down his weapon in anger, storming off into the night.

"Do not follow him, warrior," Miri put out a hand to restrain Diarmuid, who had indeed taken several steps forward. "He may go. They know the destiny he seeks, they know the fate of his unborn child were he not to succeed. They will let him stay, but the rest of us," and she turned to regard them all gathered there, "must go. Now."

And so they went, watching the misty isle of Caith Neth fade into the darkness of the sea's gloom.

XI

THE LEGENDARY

CHYMERA

"Hard to imagine anything worse than this, isn't it?"

Great was the devastation. Deep swaths of sod had been torn from the very ground, as though carved away by massive talons. Whole flocks of soft white sheep lay dead, strewn across the grassy blue hills with wild abandon. And the worst part, thought Diarmuid as he examined the slain sheep, was the fact they lay wholly intact but for their slashed throats or pierced hides. Whatever killed them had done so for sport, and not for sustenance.

The mood was grim in the long hall that night. Without their flock, Eillear had neither food nor trade with their neighbors. Samhain loomed ahead, promising the grip of a keen and dreary winter. Even Miri had descended from her hilltop oratory to join the people of Eillear in the long hall as they mournfully discussed what may become of them.

"We've enough shorn wool to keep us for some time, and fish from the Fyroe until the ice closes," their chief, Fenian, offered bracingly to the gathered villagers. Queen Niamh had been generous indeed. The boy who bore the dragon scale now ruled, with her blessing, over the valley and village of Eillear. "But we must seek out the beast that did this, and see them undone before more havoc is wrought."

Suddenly the door to the long hall flew open, admitting a shivering child whose eyes were wild with fright. He pelted himself toward the dais upon which Fenian and Aisla sat, clutching frantically at Aisla's long skirts.

"The b... the b...b.. the beast!" He chattered, favoring an arm that streamed bright with blood. In an instant Qimmirea was upon him, bathing the wound in balsam and tearing strips from the hem of her own kirtle to use as a bandage.

"Speak, child. What did this to you?" asked Aisla gently, as she lifted the child into her lap to soothe him.

"A gigantic... a bird! With the foreclaws of a lion, and the h-head of the most terrible and evil woman I ever did see! She came upon me in the wood as I was digging mushrooms - she pin me to the ground with her claws, and she screeched; oh, such a horrible screech!"

The child dissolved into wailing sobs, and Aisla stroked his head and shushed him fondly while staring wide eyed at Fenian and Diarmuid, who had joined at the dais to hear the lad's tale.

"A lion... and a bird? Do you think the boy saw a manticore?" Diarmuid asked with a lift of his eyebrow.

"But with the face of a woman? I like this not," shuddered Fenian. "So close to Samhain and the thinning of the veil, to see such wraiths as this!"

Diarmuid frowned. The boy, swallowing his sobs, motioned as though he were to speak again.

"She s... she said she... she were the wretched Chymera. That she demanded we... we feed her, a diet of... of..." he stammered, overwhelmed again by tears.

"Chymera, you said?" interrupted Miri. "No wonder she let you go with naught but a scratch."

The boy choked on another sob, and those upon the dais cast her a puzzled look. She pursed her lips and continued.

"She wants a diet of virgins, three maidens, at the end of seven days." Miri spoke matter-of-factly, crossing her arms after finishing her ministrations on the boy's wound. Then, under her breath, she added, "Why thought she to come here, before Samhain's ceremony, I cannot begin to fathom."

"But is she a chimera, or a manticore?" questioned Diarmuid in some confusion.

"She is Chymera. There are no other beasts like her, and there will never be another." Her voice lowered, her haunted tone sending shivers through the spines of those who heard it. The firelight cast eerie shadows on her face. "Chymera is the blighted spirit of the giantess Bilfulga, who once sought the hand of the King of Cait Neth."

The rest of the village listened in wide eyed wonder. Their priestess stood before the great fire in the long hall, its vivid glow flickering in the highlights of her auburn hair and shining in the depths of her expressive eyes. She held a gourd that she could either shake, and draw forth the sound of water and wind in the trees, or tap for a hollow rhythmic beat that matched the cadence of her voice. This night she used it to great effect.

"Legend says the king denied her suit, saying that he was a great and wondrous king, and he did not mean to marry but a simple giantess.

"'I need a wife who can soar,' said the King of Cait Neth, stroking the feathered head of one of the falcons with which he hunted, 'who can fly beside me as I ride my swift and noble horse.'

"'I will become as swift in flight as your falcon,' the giantess Bilfulga said boldly, 'and then, you will marry me!'

"She disappeared, seeking high in the great mountains the Andvari, who were known for their skill in smithing and mystic arts that imbued their goods with magic.

"'Can you make me a cloak of feathers,' she begged them, 'that I might soar in the sky, and hunt beside the man who will be my husband?'

"'We can do this,' said the dwarves, 'but you must promise us something in return.'

"'Anything!' she cried, pleading from her knees. 'Anything I have, or am to have, I will give to you in exchange for the cloak of feathers.'

"'In exchange for your firstborn child, be she a maiden, we will make you this cloak. Stand, and return in three days.'

"She agreed without hesitation, knowing that to her many children would be born were she to wed the great King of Cait Neth. She returned in three days, and the Andvari placed upon her shoulders the cloak of feathers.

With a single bound, she soared into the sky as swift as any falcon.

"She visited again the King of Cait Neth. 'O King,' she cried from the skies. 'I have done as you said. I can now soar alongside you as you ride your swift and noble horse.'

"The King was shocked, but shrugged. At his feet lay a cat, a beautiful long furred creature who purred delightfully. 'Surely you can soar, this is true. But I need me a wife who can sit by the fire, and warm my lap, and yet still have claws sharp enough to hunt the rats that plague our larder.'

"So she bit her lip, and she said in determination, 'I will grow claws, like the creature at your feet. And then, you will marry me!'

"Again she visited the Andvari, and again begged for their aid.

"'In exchange for your secondborn child, be she a maiden,' they said, 'we will craft you claws of unbreakable iron that you may hide when warming your husband's lap and expose to hunt the rats in the larder.'

"She agreed, and in three more days' time returned for her iron claws.

"'I have become what you asked, my lord,' she cried, as she once more begged the king for his hand in marriage.

"The king, though surprised, simply shrugged again. 'You can soar, and you can claw, but only the most beautiful maiden in all the realms,' he insisted, 'can be the one whom I will wed.'

"She grew red, with fury and with shame, but she desired the king to be her husband above all things. So she bowed, and said, 'I will become more beautiful than any maiden who came before, and any maiden that will come after, and then, surely, you will marry me.'

"'For the third time, she visited the Andvari in their forge. For the third time, she begged them to make her a wondrous item - one that would render her more beautiful than any maiden who ever lived or ever would live. And for the third time, the Andvari agreed.

"'Provided,' they said, 'your thirdborn, be she a maiden, you give up unto us. We will make you a mask of wondrous beauty. But understand,' they warned, 'these items all have great power, and they make you what you are not. You cannot wear all these items of a time together. If you do, a great curse will befall you.'

"She nodded, and as before, returned in three days' time. They gave her the mask, and she returned to the king.

"'O King,' she said, 'I have become the most beautiful maiden in the world.'

"And the king agreed, but said, with some reluctance, 'but can you fly, still?'

"She hesitated. But she drew the cloak of feathers about her shoulders and, to the king's great surprise, took flight.

"'And have you claws, then, maiden?' he asked, seeing her hands were but the normal hands of a giantess.

"She hesitated again. 'O King,' she cried. 'I can be all of these things you wish. But I cannot be all of them together. Please, I beg of you, make me your bride. And at any time I can soar like a falcon, or bear claws like a cat, or be the most beautiful maiden in the world.'

"But the king shook his head, and settled back into his throne. 'All of these things you must be, in order for me to wed you.'

"So she sighed, and she tightened the mask of great beauty, and she shifted the cloak of feathers so it settled more firmly on her shoulders, and she drew out the claws of iron.

"'I will become all of these things,' she said quietly, 'and then, you will marry me.'

"She put on the claws. With a bright flash, and a mournful wail, the giantess collapsed. On the floor before the king's throne a creature, more hideous than anything he'd ever seen, sprung from where Bilfulga had stood.

"'You have turned me into a monster!' she screeched, and the king's guard rushed to surround him, stabbing at her with their pikes and swords. With a feral scream, she soared from the throne room and over the open sea, never to be seen again on Cait Neth.

"She has since appeared on Eire," finished Miri, with an arm extended toward the fire, her eyes seeing into the depths of the past, "demanding three maidens, that she might deliver them to the Andvari and so lift the curse. But she cannot help herself. As soon as she sees the maidens, she is overcome by her fury at the hardness of the king's heart and devours them whole. She, who gave up the form of a giantess to please the king, has turned into a monster, a hybrid beast. It is said she went blind at the sight of her hideousness; tore out her own eyes with her iron claws."

The long hall grew quiet at the end of her tale. Fenian was the first to break the silence.

"Three maidens at the end of seven days. We've seven days to find this hideous creature, and slay her, before she levels our village to the ground."

Diarmuid stood, and placed his spear at Fenian's feet. "I will seek the Chymera," he said, "and with the grace of the goddess I will slay her!"

—

"Are you completely mad? You're going to fight Chymera alone?"

They had returned to the oratory - and to Miri's favorite pastime, exasperatedly browbeating the eager warrior for his reckless daring.

"None else have the strength to face her, Miri. And we haven't time to send for aid from Bjirtka or Arbannen. If I go with your blessing," he wheedled, "I won't be going quite alone."

"You're incorrigible," she said, with a frown that slowly bloomed into a smile. The dawning light of the promise of battle cast its glow upon his face and she noted how well the expression suited him, how fair he fit the profile of a legendary hero. "Alright. You have my blessing, Diarmuid," she said, dragging a finger along his cheek.

And with her blessing, he fought the Chymera.

But despite her blessing, he lost.

"She moves with all speed!" He groaned, as Qimmirea stitched shut the open wound that gaped above his brow, a gift from those iron claws.

"Were she even a moment swifter, this would've sent you to Tir na nOg. Stop moving," Miri grumbled, pressing her palms against the wounded warrior's temples to hold him steady.

"I don't get it. It's like she knows my moves before I make them. I know not how it is possible, especially since she cannot even see."

"Does she know from where you come?"

"No. I told her I was a wandering hero from a faraway land, bidden by my vow to slay a great monster in order to win my lady's hand in marriage. She seemed to like that," he smirked, "but it did not lessen her ire, nor stay the strength in those claws of hers."

"Hmm. Well, so long as she believed you she'll have no reason to attack the village again. Not until they fail to grant her three maidens."

He fell silent, playing the battle again over in his mind. Miri worked in silence, coating the stitches in a thick paste, then standing and dusting her hands on her woolen apron.

"I can remove the stitches in the morning. I assume you mean to try again?" She said, with an amused glint in her eye.

"Until the Morrigan herself calls me home," he declared, sweeping a devout glance at the stone idol, "I will face the

Chymera with my spear and my sword."

The Morrigan, though he listened keenly for her call, remained silent.

"Diarmuid!" Miri cried, as he collapsed through the doorway of the oratory three days later. He lay in a stupor the entire following day, and more than once did Miri plead with her goddess to save the soul of the wounded hero. Finally, on the morn of the sixth day since the Chymera's appearance, he roused himself fully, locking eyes with the priestess who hovered exhausted above him.

"She is still too fast," he coughed. "I fought her for three days, and three nights. I felt at times she was toying with me, or that I moved through time apart from her. I wounded her, most definitely," he said, pointing to his spear that rested against the mantelpiece, dried black blood dimming the brightness of its blade, "but I know not... I know not if I can finally defeat her."

He looked so despondent, so unhappy, it struck Miri to the heart. She laid her head upon his chest, tracing runes around the scars Chymera's claws left on his flesh. He put a hand on her hair, drawing comfort from her closeness.

"You have but one day left to face her. But, Diarmuid, my... my own strength is waning. I know not how many more times I can clutch you from the brink of death. Explain again the way she moves, and perhaps... we..."

Suddenly she trailed off, knitting her brows in consternation. He made to speak but she shushed him, pressing a finger to his mouth.

"She is blind, you said?"

"Yes. She often asks me what I look like," he swallowed uncomfortably, "she makes me describe myself in great detail."

"But you say she knows your moves? Can sense your motion, before you even make it?"

"That is so. What think you of her power, priestess?"

She breathed shallowly, collecting her thoughts as they passed quickly through her mind. "She has been blind for centuries, Diarmuid, yet she lives on; faces heroes, armies, and outwits them all. She must have... she must possess the keenest, most powerful sense of hearing. She can hear the gravel that rolls beneath your boots as you shift position, the wind that whistles along your spear with every thrust. That is how she knows your every move. And that is how she strikes before you even take a step."

"Miri. You're a genius," Diarmuid whispered. "But... what shall I do? How do I overcome this?"

She pondered again for a moment, then sat up and disappeared into her quarters. He watched her go, suddenly missing the warmth of her weight against him. But quickly she returned, entering the altar place with a bundle wrapped in her arms.

"What is that?" Diarmuid asked with great curiosity, as she stepped further into the light. She smiled, and unwrapped it deferentially.

It was a great horn, carved with wondrous detail. "It's been a long time since I've blown this," she said, as she dusted the horn with a gentle stroke.

"Blow… What?"

She looked at him severely, her lip twitching. "Focus, Diarmuid. The beast is keen of hearing. Blow upon this wondrous horn, and it will distract her, confuse her senses, and give you an opportunity to strike. But you understand," she said with emphasis, "you must draw a mighty breath. For if the horn dies for even a moment, she will regain her hearing and slay you where you stand."

He opened his mouth, then closed it at the sight of her forbidding look. Meekly, he took the horn and slung it across his chest.

"I will take the horn and face her on the morrow," he promised. "Will I have your blessing again, priestess?"

She raised an eyebrow suggestively. "Perhaps. I could teach you how to blow that horn with only a single breath, for starters."

—

At the dawn of the seventh day, he enters for the third time the ancient forest in which dwelt the great Chymera. She slinks from her cave, and a smile blooms on the ravages of her terrible face.

"Hero. You've returned again, I see," she hisses. "I wonder if the bride you seek is the Morrigan herself."

He made no answer. He was taking deep, measured breaths, filling his lungs in preparation for battle.

"What, speechless today? That's too bad. I will miss the sound of your voice when I draw the last drop of blood from your veins!"

She poised to strike. Diarmuid drew a mighty breath, brought the horn to his lips, and blew.

She shrieked, pivoting in place and screwing up her monstrous face in agony. As he blew, he thrust with the spear, digging it deep into the monster's side.

"Cease that infernal sound! You trickster! You fiend!" She screeched, swiping her deadly claws at his face.

But now that her senses of hearing are dulled she moves not as swiftly, nor with the clairvoyance she was wont to show in times before. He easily outmaneuvers her, stabbing again and again into her flanks and chest with his mighty spear. With each thrust she grows weaker, her attacks less powerful. Through it all Diarmuid holds that mighty blast upon the horn.

Finally she collapses. With the tip of his spear, he severs the cord that tied the cloak of feathers around her neck. With a stroke of his sword, he cuts off the fingers that bore the claws of iron. And finally, with his own hands, he lifts the mask of great beauty, that had become terrible and horrifying with the giantess' curse.

She gave a great wail and slowly collapsed. Her monstrous form disintegrated, and in its place lay the curled corpse of the giantess Bilfulga.

"Be at peace, giantess," prayed Diarmuid, tossing the cursed Andvari objects into the depths of the dark and ancient forest. "No longer will you be haunted by your curse. May we meet again in the halls of Tir na nOg."

Over her lifeless body he built a cairn marked with a flat white stone, into which he carved her name: Bilfulga, the

Unloved. With a final salute, he turned and left the forest.

—

Samhain night, when the veil between the worlds is thinnest. The priestess, Miri, dances in delight before a roaring bonfire. She is naked, clothed only in ropes of glittering glass beads from which bones and the skulls of small beasts hang. She is the only one who moves in this sacred space.

The villagers range before her as she performs her deep and spiritual ritual of the night. She calls forth the souls long gone before to meet the mortals, their kin, who they left behind. Their bodies sit before the bonfire, but their spirits dance beyond the veil.

Diarmuid watches, his spear crossed over his chest. He does not seek to cross the veil this night. The Morrigan watches her flock, smiles as they wander among the living, reminding them of the wonder and glory that it is to be dead. He senses her, but he seeks her not. He is still shy of her, knows better than to weary his welcome at her glorious feet. She will call him one day, he knows this. He need only wait.

A light, dancing from the glowing fire, makes its way toward him. He thinks it is an ember until it blooms, and grows, and takes the form of a woman - a giantess, noble in bearing and sweet of face. She smiles, and he suddenly knows her.

"Bilfulga. I see you have found your way beyond the veil," he said, and bowed in greeting.

"I have. I wanted to greet the hero who saved me - releasing my soul from the misery of that hateful curse.

I thank you, noble warrior," and she dipped low in
gratitude before him.

"You owe me no thanks. You are strong, and beautiful,
Bilfulga. I can only be sorry the King did not see that, or
value you at your worth," he replied sadly and earnestly.

But she laughed. "I have long since forgiven the King
of Cait Neth. He may not have known my worth, but I
should have known it myself. And I should not have tried
in vain to change who I was to suit his desires, for all
know how futile an effort that truly is. Always know your
own worth. For those who appreciate it," she advised,
with a wise look toward the priestess who still danced
before the fire, "will come to you."

Before he could reply, she waved and vanished, passing
again through the veil from this world to the one beyond.

He blinked. Before him the embers lay dying, the bonfire
long spent; the villagers returned to house and hearth,
and he alone remained with the ghosts of the past.

Alone but for Miri, who sat beside him, the spirits of the
dead still dancing in the depths of her eyes.

XII

TO WAR

"You're going off to war?"

She was hanging linens on a clothesline in the brief, mellow afternoon sun. But she stopped long enough to stare forbiddingly at him. His face, cast in shadow, was an enigma.

They screamed in the streets, beat their breasts and dusted their uncovered heads in dirt. King Hrothgir lay in state, the bloody wound in his throat sewn shut by the steady hands of Arbannen's noble druids.

Our King was murdered. And only vengeance could wash away our grief.

"Yes. Prince Darothil himself will lead us north, to drown the barbarians of the fens in their own blood. They had no right to spill ours, and they must pay for it with theirs, or never will King Hrothgir's soul rest in peace in our Lady's Hall. The Bjirtka priests themselves have blessed his holy calling."

She scoffed under her breath. He knew her feelings about the holy men that had come to Bjirtka, and the edicts they passed down as law from the words of their new god. More and more often they called for acts of valor, for raids and victory to prove devotion. She could forgive the profligacies of Niamh's divine maidens - though they too claimed divinity covered a multitude of sins, they at least drew the line at wanton and unmitigated bloodshed. But raids against the godless heathens outside of Eire (and even sometimes within it) that did little more to bring its people closer to their beloved deities than fill the church's coffers and spill their own blood, increased almost daily.

And none knew better than she the fate of the unshriven warriors whose bodies rotted on foreign beaches.

"If I go with them, I can at least be sure they return home," he insisted. *Alive or dead. No matter their cause, I won't leave them to fall alone.*

"So that's your noble duty, then? To lead strangers in a stranger's battle, for naught more than glory and gold?"

He had the grace to look hurt. "I thought I would leave with your blessing."

A breeze rippled the linens hanging on the lines. They both smelled the rain it carried. A brief afternoon clarity spoiled by yet another storm.

"You thought wrongly."

"Miri..."

"No! What good will it do you? You fight for men, not the gods. If you say our Lady's blessing has come to you from other lips, then what import do mine have?"

He sighed exasperatedly. "You have such high standards for all around you, Miri. You know not the damage you do to the people who know they'll never measure up."

"Why shouldn't I have, then," she demanded, arms crossed over her chest. "I hold myself to those same standards. You think you're the only one who struggles with expectations of greatness and perfection?"

He gestured impatiently. "But it's so easy for you. You admit your flaws so freely."

He saw a fire kindled in the depths of her eyes, and almost he wished he'd swallowed his words.

"You have no idea of my weaknesses, Diarmuid. You see my strengths, you watch me heal you time and again, and you think because I am able to do so that my talent comes with ease - comes without the darkness and fear that fills my every waking moment." She winced, and hesitated before saying almost under her breath, "You think it easy? To watch you leave and know not when or if you'll return? Think I don't writhe and rail at myself in some kind of misguided belief I've driven you away, for once, for good?"

He flinched, but looked grave. "You know the Lady I serve, Qimmirea. I do her bidding, same as you."

She threw her arms out at her sides, pain and frustration clear in her face. "You claimed to know my flaws. I do my job because without it I am nothing. And if I must suffer for being alive, I might as well turn that suffering to some purpose. My goddess sends me heroes in benediction, in praise of my skill and my devotion, but she knows not..." she choked, "she knows not the mortal heart she wounds."

He stared at her bemusedly, not recognizing in this tortured and spiteful being the good natured, kind, humorous priestess of the Morrigan; a woman he'd come to admire as a sort of manifestation of the Lady herself, in all her wisdom, and generosity, and keen empathy.

She was only human, after all.

"The treasure and glory we seek is for the goddess," he insisted softly. "You think yourself above reproach, but I don't see you turning down her gifts and blessings either, no matter," he gestured at himself carelessly, "the form they take."

As soon as he spoke the words he wished them unsaid. He knew they were unfair. He cursed himself, even as her face turned white as death.

"Leave. Now."

"Miri, I..."

"No. Leave."

Without giving him another chance to speak, she stormed off. He thought about following her, but the rain had begun to fall. So he pulled down her laundry, folding it meticulously in the basket she'd left behind.

And he left for war.

—

Is your hair growing longer, she wonders, as his mouth opens in a feral scream, his blade tearing through the heart of an enemy soldier. She wanders through the forest, plucking mushroom caps and listening to the rain mist on the canopy overhead as he stumbles in the mud, pulling free a spear tangled in the spine of a slain warrior and throwing it with deadly force through the belly of another. All around him are the groans of dying men. The women and children had gone silent long ago.

Do you hear the call of your goddess? He stands to stare at the battlefield, raising the axe he'd buried in his opponent's skull after tearing it from the man's grip. She watches as the mournful red sun sets on the horizon. He inhales the sharp smell of metallic blood, tasting it between his teeth. Her brow furrows as a murder of hoarse crows tumbles through the sky.

As she closes her eyes in prayer, he opens his, wipes them clear of dirt and the viscera of his enemies. Her voice carries on the wind. A kulning cry, one of the old songs. Its flat, but sweet tone carries to the ears of her goddess. The Lady's own voice swells to a din as she calls them, the warriors who fall on the battlefield, one after the other after the other.

Is there hope still lurking in your heart?

Men collapse in pools of blood, their cries of agony drowned out by her incessant call, her sweet promise. She will carry them home. They need not fear death, not when she is so beautiful. He drags their bodies from where they fall to the boats that line the beach. Their pockets are full of gold, trinkets, baubles. Their eyes are empty.

Life does not have to be strife and torment in order for it to have meaning.

—

Before the winding horns reached the valley, before the heralds cried the triumphant return of the warriors from Eillear, she sensed him. The Morrigan had sent her hero back.

The dull gold of his hair shone in the sun. He came up

through the austere stone piles that marked her oratory's entrance, a sign that he felt unsure of his reception. Most preferred to visit through the kitchen garden instead of the graveyard, and he was no exception.

Her presence at the doorway surprised him. Perhaps he misjudged his welcome. As he approached, he reached for her hand, but she withdrew it, recoiling at his daring.

"Don't. Do not touch me right now. I may regret it in a minute but right now I do not want you here. You can't just leave like that, and come back like this, and I don't know what you expect, but I am sure... I'm sure I can't give it to you."

A crow went wheeling through the clear and humid mid-afternoon sky. Clear but for a single storm cloud resting on the horizon. Without waiting for a response, without waiting to see if he'd leave or stay, she pinched the bridge of her nose between her fingers and took one deep breath, then two, before walking away.

Fail me, my Lady. Take this all away. I've nothing to reproach myself for but being a fool, a fool, a fool.

When she stepped out the next morning, she tripped over his boots. He had to catch her to prevent her from tumbling ignominiously over her own threshold.

"You didn't leave."

"I didn't," he replied cautiously.

"Why?"

"I didn't want to."

Neither of them knew what to say to that.

—

"It's war. What would you want to know of it?"

A single candle split the gloom. They sat on opposite ends of the grainy wood table. But their bodies, leaning almost imperceptibly in towards one another, belied their posturing stiffness.

"Did we win?"

He snorted, unable to hide the smile caused by her frank question. "King Hrothgir has been avenged. His son Darothil has no reason to fear the safety of his throne. Whether Bjirtka's priests let him keep it is another story, but one I haven't the knowledge tell you."

She drummed her fingertips on the tabletop. His scalp crinkled - not at the sound her chipped, uneven nails made against the wood but in memory of how they felt brushing through his hair. He wondered idly how many gifts she'd received since he was gone. Then he realized it didn't matter. Nothing really mattered apart from the fact he was once again under her roof, enjoying her company. He couldn't even bring himself to be shocked at the thought.

Suddenly he caught himself leaning forward, and began to straighten, but stopped and laughed at himself under his breath. She watched closely, then in one swift motion got up and buried him in a fierce hug.

"I missed you," she said, her face in his hair. "I didn't want to miss you but, there it is. And the thought of some other dirty hedge witch shrivening your corpse;

preparing your lifeless body for its journey to the Morrigan, it... well..."

He squeezed her softly. She didn't need to finish.

"Come," he whispered, and stood, lifting her in his firm grasp. "You owe me a blessing, priestess."

A faint blush stole across her face, but she didn't deny him. They left the kitchen to kneel at the altar, but something in the impassive stone face of the idol gave them pause.

"No," she said, turning towards him with a look in her eyes that made his knees weak. "We do not need to seek the goddess. She has already granted us her benediction. I want you, and only you, to fill my heart and soul this night."

They barely make it to her couch. As they tumble naked onto the furs they seem to clutch one another like a drowning man clutches to the sandy bank of the river. He pulls her into his lap, lifting her arching back, filling her with more than just his heart and his soul. His mouth finds her breast and she moans in pleasure, wrapping her fingers in his hair, curling herself around him and squeezing him with her thighs.

He calls not on the goddess. He calls on her instead, breathing her name in her ear, liking the way it sent a thrill throughout her body to hear his low and sincere tones begging for her blessing. He strokes her flesh, feeling her goosebumps, her heartbeat. He touches the heat between her legs with his fingers and watches in delight as her face contorts in absolute bliss.

There was meaning to life, after all. She shudders beneath

him, alternately panting and calling upon her great power to bless him. He listens to the old tongue as it flows across her lips, her accent punctuated by cries of wonder and ecstasy. He slows for a moment and she lays him down, then straddles his hips, and he cries her name again with a feeling more beautiful than any he's ever known in his heart.

It is love. It is selfish, it is foolish, it is mortal, it is love.

Spent, they collapse breathlessly onto the couch, tangled in blankets and furs and one another. He looks at the moonlight shining on the softness of her tousled hair, feels the heat of her breath against his collarbone, and she can see that same moonlight reflected in the blue of his softened eyes. Deep within him is a sense of calm, of peace, the kind he only ever experiences when he is around her.

"Diarmuid," she said, tracing runes with her finger on his bare chest. "You don't owe me anything. You know that."

Of course he did. He kissed the top of her head, breathing deep the smell of her. "I don't need to owe you anything, Qimmirea. I find myself in you. I follow the call of the Morrigan - but you give that call meaning, give my fruitless chase a sense of purpose."

She was quiet. She knew the gods were listening. She felt the weight of divinity, the grace in which she'd walked for a century or more, settle within her. She knew not when she would hear the Morrigan's call for herself, but she knew that until she did, the space she filled would have value and reason. The sound of her name on his lips thrilled her to the tips of her toes. The sight of him here, in her bed, reminded her that perhaps the gods do temper their judgements with mercy.

They lay like that 'til dawn. Sometimes, it is enough to just simply be.

—

She presided over a mass funeral the next moon. The entire village of Eillear had travelled to Bjirtka to honor the warriors who would be buried beside the king for whose honor and vengeance they fell.

And so the mounds were raised, and so the people watched as the greatest king they would ever know was laid to rest, chests of gold at his feet and his favored battle axe clutched in his firm grip. The ravens circled, and they felt with reverence the call of the Morrigan as it surrounded them - in the chanting voice of Miri, the wandering druids of Arbannen, and the elders of their tribe who took up her voice with their own. A keening cry in the old tongue, that the old ways might not truly die with this most beloved king.

For the old ways would die one day, as did the ways before them. And so will the ways after, for the lives of men are short.

But for now they sang in reverence and feasted in plenty, for the death of the king meant the bounty of his benevolence would be spread among all who loved and owed fealty to him. Though off-put by the presence of Bjirtka's holy priests, who prayed in such strange ways over the feast, and the strange customs observed by their prince, which they had never seen before and knew not how to imitate, the funeral remained joyous; a cause for celebration as much as for grief.

Diarmuid noticed quickly that Miri had not taken a place

at the board. Just as quickly, when a priest breathing of
wine and sour benediction tried to pray over his meal,
did he realize why she bothered not to remain at the feast.
The holy men had known to steer clear of her pagan ritual
as she laid the soul of the late king to rest - but it went not
without a fight.

"You think you can... what do you call it... 'baptize'
the corpse of your father in the name of a god he never
knew? Darothil, I've humored your whims for now, as I
know one day you will be my king. But today is not that
day, and I will not let you so disrespect your father,"
she seethed, when summoned to the throne room by the
prince.

"You cannot dictate to me in my own hall, priestess,"
he spat, but she saw in the depths of his eyes a fear that
fanned the flames of her ire.

"She can, Prince Darothil, and she will, when your word
has not the weight of your father's and your rule is not
yet recognized."

The druid of Arbannen, sent to the funeral as an honorary
envoy of Queen Niamh, spoke softly. But the threat in her
voice was clear. Arbannen worshiped the old gods and
rebuffed these so-called sacred men who had come from
the south bearing word of a new and almighty deity that
dared to transcend above theirs.

He swallowed, a sour expression on his face. But he could
see surrounding him in greater number than the holy
priests, and his own faithful thanes, the old warriors who
swore fealty to his father and who would be hard-pressed
to swear fealty to him were he to desecrate the old king's
grave.

"Do as you will, then, priestess," he scoffed, sweeping majestically and none-too-steadily from the throne upon which he sat.

In the depths of Miri's eyes there was a sadness and a resignation that Diarmuid had only ever seen at a graveside. Though she'd held the ceremony with grace, and tact, and though he knew beyond a doubt his leader's soul lived again in the fabled land of Tír na nÓg, he could see still in her eyes that same grief as he approached her where she sat on a small hill overlooking the bay of Bjirtka.

Twilight spread its amethyst gloom upon the quiet seaside town. A soft wind tousled the dry grasses, carrying with it frigid salty spray from the ocean. She hugged her knees tightly to her chest and kept her face half-hidden in her folded arms, her bright eyes wet and glowing with the sky that colored them.

Those eyes watched him as he approached and silently seated himself beside her. Those eyes closed, slowly, as she leaned against his broad shoulder. He reached a hand out to wipe a tear from her cheek.

"He is where... he always longed to be," Diarmuid's tone was low, and heartfelt, though he knew not the words to use to soothe the melancholy priestess.

"He is. We should be grateful. If only we all would be so lucky one day, right?" She too spoke softly, carefully, as though measuring each sound before she uttered it.

Frogs sang in the marshes as night fell in earnest. The sounds of merriment floated up from the town; ghostly, haunting, echoing as they did among the sand hills and dunes surrounding the bay. A lone gull wound

its keening cry through the darkened sky, answered
by chittering birds who sought nest and brush and the
safety of shelter. Miri dug her bare feet into the sandy
earth, feeling its grit between her toes as she often felt it
between her fingers when tossing handfuls of dirt into the
graves of the men and women she buried.

"To earth we all return. May our hearts become food for
worms," she chuckled dismally.

"So long as you haven't lost it during life, is that it?"
Diarmuid joked back lightly.

"Is that a hint?" She replied with her crooked smile.
"You're so interested in the nature of my relationship with
our departed king, Diarmuid."

"Well... can't I be?" He asked defensively.

She laughed softly. "Of course I loved the king. I also
loved the king's wife. It broke my heart when she died.
Brynhilde and Valka were beauties, but they were nothing
compared to Hildegard."

She stared, misty-eyed, at the moon rising above the bay.
He swallowed. "What did Hildegard do, that made the...
the *bean feasa* curse her?"

Miri's eyes flashed, but her playful grin wrinkled the
bridge of her nose. "That was not a *bean feasa*. That was
a fae. Hildegard went to a wise woman for a philter of
beauty that would win her a king for a mate, and a fae
tried to trick her into giving up the philter to it instead.
Luckily Hildegard had brains as well as beauty, but she
made the dire mistake," and Miri's brow furrowed, "of
mocking the fae, and bragging about her triumph, in the
markets of Bjirtka after she'd wedded the king."

"How could the fae know? And... wait, how did a philter make Hildegard so beautiful that Hrothgir wedded her?"

Miri laughed. "Hrothgir already loved her. Hildegard simply didn't believe it. Part of me thinks she was jealous of the wise woman, for she knew of the king's trust in her and of the nature of rituals performed by priestesses and heroes of the Morrigan."

Diarmuid blushed. "Do you mean... so you and Hrothgir..."

"Don't ask if you don't want to know," she warned lightly.

"Fine. Go on."

Miri smiled, leaning more comfortably on Diarmuid's shoulder. "Hildegard came to the wise woman for a philter of beauty; at least, that was her professed claim. But when she saw her, she realized she had nothing to fear of the king's fidelity were he to wed. And she learned too, that no bastard child," Miri spoke lightly, but there was constraint in her tone that gave Diarmuid pause, "could be born of any clandestine union were he not as faithful as he proclaimed. Of course, I made her the philter anyways," Miri laughed, "because she paid me, and by doing so we had sealed a kind of unspoken agreement between ourselves; that of mistress and of merchant, one that could not be broken by ill feeling or distrust. And she often came to me too, when the sickness that ate away at her grew to be more than she could bear."

"And you could not lift the curse on her children?"

Her face grew very sad. "I could not. I cannot break the bond of the fae. Hildegard knew it, and she should have done more to make certain her children knew it, too. I never let Valka find me, and Gewinna, rest her soul, tried her best to convince the child that the priestess of Eillear was not the hag who'd cursed her at her cradle. She knew not the child would seek other means to unveil her fate, and I do regret that I had not done more to stop her. But what others weave I cannot unravel, and fate," she sighed, looking at Diarmuid seriously, "is something I will never try to change."

They sat in silence for a moment, before Miri continued. The starry sky had supplanted the twilight ombré of azure into peony pinks and lavender hues, and a slender new moon hung among the glowing river of the uncharted universe above.

"As for how the fae knew of Hildegard's shameless bragging, well, they heard her themselves. She'd gone to market, same as she'd always done, though her first time as queen. I don't think she knew well how to assume a place above the people she'd grown up with as an equal. And perhaps in trying to give them a reason more than her new title to respect her, she got a little garrulous in defending her actual accomplishments. It just happened to be a bad day to do it; for the fae, learning of Bjirtka's new queen, had come to the market themselves to most likely work some mischief or nonsense, as they do."

Diarmuid shivered. "I can't imagine how it would have been to meet a fae in such a place. What appearance had they?"

She smiles, and her expression grows dreamy as she looks back into the distant past. The slim columns of gray stone that rise in a circle atop the grassy hill; the squares of cloth, spread out in abundance, over which items of great variety are tossed. The rising and falling voices of merchants, butchers, hawkers of wares from near and far and the bustle of patrons who grope for pennies or goods of their own to exchange. The dancing of maidens at the whimsical music that seemed to pervade the marketplace, and the feats of strength and daring performed by men who sought notoriety and fame. The tall and beautiful queen who walks slowly with her retinue of waiting women, tossing flowers and coins to the children who watch as she passes and wave at the sight of her dazzling smile.

She sees all this, and she sees too a group of five women wearing veils and speaking only in hushed whispers wandering the market at will. Most give them a wide berth, though strangers are infrequent in this town where everyone knows everyone. They do not draw off their veils and they do not speak to any but themselves. But they listen. They hear the queen as she speaks of her triumph over one of their own, knowing not that they are listening, caring not they mean to seek revenge.

"The fae have lost much of the power they hold over this land. They no longer have anywhere to hide, and their vicious and devious natures do them no favors. One day they, too, will vanish," she finished, and breathed deeply, idly twisting the claddagh she wore on her rightmost index finger, "along with the old gods, and the magic that weaves itself through Eire."

"And you wonder why the king, and... well, others like him... seek death with such a burning desire," nudged Diarmuid, as he scowled at the idea of magic and the gods leaving the land he loved so much.

"I don't wonder, Diarmuid. I'm a priestess of Death. I

know the pull of her siren call. But passing on from this world to the next does not halt the change that comes. You can either avoid it, or you can guide it, and grow with it, and hope that what comes after has as much beauty as that which came before."

She too wore a scowl, though. He realized she must be thinking of the priests; Darothil's holy men who all but threatened to kill the gods themselves.

As they watch, ghostly figures dance upon the beach with wild abandon. One day it will be them. But today is not that day.

XIII

DREAD PLAGUE

She had over her face a cone of stitched leather, and on her hands she wore gloves of pigskin. Looking out from her eyes was the saddest expression he'd ever seen in them.

"It's a plague. None may leave the village unless I say so, you understand?"

Aisla nodded fearfully, then jumped as she noticed Diarmuid's approach. He saw that she, too, wore a mask; one of cloth, though her hands were bare and coated in a shiny paste.

"A plague? Are you sure?" He asked.

"Yes. Her fever is high, but she shivers and fights for every breath, and says she tastes no food that crosses her lips. I know not who brought it, nor how long ago, but I have only the shortest time until the whole village is struck."

"The children. We must get them out of the village. But where will they go?" Aisla's face was white, but she spoke with clarity and purpose despite the sister who lay dying before her.

Miri paused, thinking swiftly. She looked up at Diarmuid.

"Arbannen. If we are early, they may have aid for us.

You must take two men. Wash thoroughly in the hottest waters you can tolerate." She handed him a jar of a strong smelling unguent. It burned his nose, like the strongest sip of spirits he'd ever drunk. "Before you touch anything, cover your hands in this and wait for a few moments. Niamh will never forgive me if I bring plague to her city, but everyone will die without her help."

She bustled around the oratory, desperate to ease the dying pangs of the woman on her altar while also detailing the village's needs. "Cloth and wood, for makeshift homes to separate the healthy from the sick. Tallow and lye, for soap to wash clean the lingering illness. Alcohol, spirits, as much as they can spare."

The patient was Gerthe. She gasped and moaned on the couch, her skin tinged a sickening grey-blue. He could hear the death rattle in her throat already. His heart sank at the sight of her, her belly swollen with child against her woolen dress, her feverish gaze that could fix on nothing in this life and instead looked fretfully into the beyond.

Aisla, too, stared mournfully at her pregnant sister. "Fenian told me a tale once of how he saved the life of a lamb by cutting it from its dead mother's belly. Can not the same be done for my sister's child?"

"You are asking for an ill magic, girl," warned Miri. But she put a hand on Gerthe's swollen stomach and felt the life that dwindled inside of it. She sighed.

"Diarmuid, your knife please. I... haven't a steady hand right now. I will show you where to cut."

He nodded, and with a swift, sure stroke followed with his knife the line she drew with her fingers. He was rewarded with a weak, but healthy cry as the child was lifted from its mother's womb. With a faint sigh, Gerthe smiled, casting one single look of recognition at her baby, before closing her eyes forever.

Miri wrapped it gently in an altar cloth, the cleanest and the closest she had on hand. She passed the bundle to Aisla, who stood waiting to bathe the child.

"You must watch him closely. Put him in a pot and leave him as near to the oven as you can get. He is early, and his blood is slow, but should he survive the night he perhaps will have a fighting chance. A greater one than his poor mother."

"He is a boy?" Breathed Aisla, as she cuddled him close to her breast.

"Yes. Name him, quickly, for if he dies unshriven I shudder to think of the fate of his or Gerthe's soul." Miri spoke fearfully, a tone Diarmuid had never heard in her usually confident voice.

Aisla looked long at them both. "Diarmuid. Gerthe always... May I name him Diarmuid?"

The warrior nodded with a sideways glance at Miri. Smiling thankfully, Aisla left to care for the baby Diarmuid.

Miri began to wrap the body slowly, anointing her forehead and chin with oils. As she worked, Diarmuid noticed her hands were shaking.

"The babe is not mine, Miri."

She laughed under her breath. "I didn't ask. But the boy now has... quite a name to live up to."

"You think I should have denied Aisla's request?"

"What I think matters not, least of all to you."

She doesn't know how much her words sting. But then, she's wondering if taking the life of the mother in order to save the life of the son won't lose her favor with the goddess. The Morrigan would never be so cruel.

"You should go. Bring the men to me first so that I can check to be sure they take no fever to Arbannen. And then, Diarmuid, you must take every healthy woman, man, and child to the forest," she insisted. "To the far heights of the Fyroe. There, upstream, you should be safe."

"And you?" He knew her answer, but wanted her to say it to him. If she believed she didn't need him, he wanted to hear it from her own lips.

"I stay here. Heal those I can heal, and burn the bodies of those I can't."

"Alone?"

"Yes, Diarmuid. Alone. It's my job, and I'm very good at it."

Her hands were still shaking. He wanted to hold them. He wanted to throw her on the back of the swiftest horse he could find and ride from here, from plagues, from the wrath of gods.

Instead he took the bundle she'd packed for him and left for Arbannen.

He knew they were too late by the crowds that surrounded Arbannen's gates. The bridge, drawn up to stem the influx of travelers who begged to cross the moat into the safety of the city, had been peppered with arrows and knives and axes, the weapons of desperate folk who pleaded in vain for aide.

He noticed among the men were strangers. They bore a crest, a red rose atop a black cross, and they moved with the fierce discipline of soldiers. Standing with them were men he recognized; the holy priests who had come to Bjirtka and so influenced the new rule of Bjirtka's prince.

"Should we turn 'round, then? No telling whether these folk carry the dread disease themsel'," spoke one of the men who accompanied Diarmuid.

He sighed. He knew sight of him would cause Niamh to lower her drawbridge. But he knew too that the crazed horde might take advantage of the temporary opening.

"I will go meet one of the lesser guardsmen, see if word can't be brought to the Queen of the aid we seek. Wait in the long hall of Ua Craite. I'll return by nightfall."

The Queen's guards were easily sought. He dispatched one and waited impatiently in the underbrush of the forest that encircled Arbannen. But before the sun had fully set, two robed figures approached silently.

"You are empty handed," Diarmuid noted, a dull note of finality in his voice.

"We have naught to give, mighty hero. The plague has stricken all within a hundred leagues of here. That which we have we gave away; it is all we can do to hold out against the illness ourselves," the druid replied mournfully.

He saw the fearful look she cast toward the crowd surrounding the castle.

"Who are those men? I thought Niamh denied the holy priests entry into the realm of Arbannen," Diarmuid asked.

The sisters tightened their hands into fists, and their cold eyes grew fierce. "They have a different demand of our queen now."

"I take it Queen Niamh is loath to recognize Darothil's rule?" He prodded.

"And do you blame her? To let such men as these guide him… turn him and his people from the gods of their fathers, and their fathers before them? To blame this plague, and the failing crops," she said, throwing her hands up in disgust, "on witches who defy nature, and the natural order of things. What do they know of nature? They tear up the forests, they level mountains and turn the earth to ash beneath the pounding hooves of their mighty steeds."

She pursed her mouth, cutting off her own tirade with a sharp intake of breath. Her sister placed a hand on her shoulder. A hand, Diarmuid noted, that shook.

The sisters were not simply angry. They were fearful.

"What do we do?" He asked gently. "The threat they pose is nothing in comparison to the threat of plague. We must be able to go somewhere, do something."

The druid turned her amethyst eyes on her sister. She

thought for a moment, then spoke.

"There is a hidden wood not far from here that borders your Fyroe. Within it the Queen's ancestors once held an ancient stronghold. Though untouched for a hundred years, you may find safety and shelter in its walls. A haven for your healthy, to protect them as long as this dread plague lasts."

"And a cure? Is there one?"

The druids narrowed their eyes at the desperation in his voice. "The Morrigan is angry. We know well who drew down her wrath, warrior," she said, turning a cold look at the flashing plate of the soldiers who stood outside Arbannen's high walls, "And until she is appeased, this plague will spread."

With that, they turned and swept back toward the city, leaving Diarmuid alone in the darkening wood.

Aisla met him on the outskirts of Eillear, her face falling as she saw they returned empty handed. But she brightened quickly as he explained the hidden stronghold, and with the rest, the healthy villagers who had received Qimmirea's blessing to escape, they left the valley.

He looked back once to the trees that sheltered the oratory on the hill. He saw only a slender column of smoke. Nothing more.

Inactivity ill suited the menfolk, who grumbled angrily about a foe they could not see and therefore could not fight. The women sat in huddled groups, nursing children with fear and unrest in their dull eyes. They raged at the gods who would so abandon them; lay silent as their people died.

Diarmuid too chafed against the bonds of self-imposed
exile. He took the men hunting. But in this, the dead
of winter, little game could be found. He strove far for
tidings of the plague, slathering himself with the slowly
dwindling contents of Miri's jug of salve before riding out
to the keeps of Arbannen and Bjirtka, the proud towns
of Vardrfjord and Ua Craite, and even venturing into the
fens where sulked the defeated men of Odinn's tribe.

On the roads he met none but the towering pyres of
burning bodies. In the towns he saw only the sullen and
haunted eyes of the living, who waited for the Morrigan's
inevitable call.

One night Aisla came across him crouched over the
dwindling embers of the hall's peat fire. A look of defeat
bowed his shoulders, and he hid eyes full of tears in the
hands that so often summoned death. She cleared her
throat quietly at the end of the long hall, alerting him
to her presence before disturbing him in a moment of
weakness. He looked up and beckoned her to his side.

"Waiting is not my strong suit," he said, smiling tightly,
not at all ashamed of the trace of tears that lingered in his
palms.

"Now you know the strength of women, who wait at
home for their men to return from war," she replied
simply, seating herself next to him. "You've heard
nothing, then?"

"Nothing. Arbannen's gates are still shut. Prince Darothil
and his men seem to have drawn down the wrath of the
gods, and of Queen Niamh. All the rest lies in ashes."
He remembered the pyres, the towers of smoke, the ever

present stench of death.

She held her hands over the dying embers, stretching her long fingers. He noticed they were mottled with patches of lingering dye, marked as though she had spent the day mixing draughts and salves of her own.

"Did Miri teach you to make the unguent that protects from the plague?"

"She did. Of late she's taught me many things. Our good priestess will not take an apprentice, but even she knows she cannot live forever, and must leave her knowledge with someone. It's hard to find what's necessary for her medicines here though. This place may be well protected from the harshness of winter, but most things lay still dormant under the frost. I promised I would do all I could, and this is the best I can offer."

She sighed, knitting her brows suddenly in frustration. He looked at her questioningly.

"If I told you there were a legendary panacea, to cure all ills… would you believe me?" She said frankly, in response to his gaze.

"All legends are born from the seeds of truth," he responded, his eyes already aglow with the possibility. "What legend can you tell of such a thing?"

She folded her hands, and assumed a look of deep concentration. "It was long ago. Before I came to Eillear, there were tales among the Sami people who once traded with clan Rodval, before…" she winced, then continued. "They told of a creature who encircled the Earth, who grew so long and so old that his beginning and end were one in the same. The creature is a serpent, and that serpent's name is Jormungandr."

She seemed to fall into a trance, recalling the wonderful
tale from her youth - the tale of a land, far to the north,
where the ice never melts. In that land there lived a sea
serpent, a real one, whose maw was full of vicious teeth.
And those teeth were full of venom; a venom that can
cure all ills.

"If you seek Jormungandr, there's no telling when you
may return home. The land of Everwinter is far. Farther
even than Prince Darothil's holy men, who claim to have
seen the sands of the mystic men to the south and the
misty green forests to the west, have gone. Could you
leave us for so long, then, perhaps never to return?"

The words unspoken hovered in the air. *Could you leave
her here to never know your fate? Seek the call of your goddess
without taking leave of the priestess who saved your very soul?*

"You know I must, Aisla. If there is any truth to this magic
venom, I will find it out myself. I will go to Jormungandr
in the land of Everwinter, and I will tear the teeth that
bear the poison from his mouth with my own hands."

She knew he must. That's why she'd told him the tale,
after all.

"Go, then. Let us hope you return, and not to a barren
land laid to waste by plague."

And so, he went.

—

The wind blew ceaselessly. And though ice lay all around
him, the wind blew dry. His lips cracked and every

exposed inch of skin chafed.

He felt it not.

The undulating landscape spread out before him, and what he once took for rocks, nondescript mounds in the distance, upon closer inspection bore the mark of scales. Jormungandr, the great serpent. Whether the beast were truly long enough to wrap around the Earth remained irrelevant. Only the serpent's head mattered.

For in his maw lay teeth. And in his teeth dripped venom. Venom with the fabled power to cure all ills. Diarmuid didn't need to cure all of them. He just needed to cure one.

Though the sun had yet to fully rise, he realized it already began its descent along the wasted horizon. As he walked, he suddenly came across a group of tents of skin and fur. The people who stirred among them were few; massive and shaggy, though perhaps that was simply the furs they'd wrapped around themselves for warmth in this desolate land. They brought to bear weapons made of wood and bone, but they did not attack. They simply stood and watched the lone warrior climb the ridgeback into the Arctic north, where slept the great serpent Jormungandr.

He sees the beast's yellow eyes. It watches as he approaches, drawing forth the spear slung across his back. Those yellow eyes narrow. That great serpentine head rises from the pile of frozen rock upon which it rests. Though he cannot see it he hears the moan of the sea, locked beneath ice fathoms deep.

"You are bold to come this far, warrior," hissed the great beast.

"Are you Jormungandr?" He responded, "Jormungandr, the great serpent whose maw is full of teeth, and whose teeth are full of venom?"

"I am he," said the serpent. "And I can say with utmost confidence, warrior, that you will not leave from here alive."

"We'll see in whose confidence the Morrigan invests her notice then," Diarmuid spat in return.

The great serpent rears back his mighty head, striking with surety at Diarmuid. Three strikes, the viper's head snapping forward with lightning quick recoils. The serpent tastes blood and smiles viciously.

That is, until he realized it was his own blood he tasted.

"Fiend! What man are you that moves so quickly?!" He screeches as black venom and bright red blood leak from his fanged maw. "You should be dead, and yet here you stand!"

"I am Diarmuid, once of the Fianna and Morrigan's mightiest hunters, now of Eillear and the warriors who uphold the might of Eire. I am Diarmuid, and until the Morrigan calls for me," he said, shoulders thrown back in defiance and a dripping fang ripped from the mouth of the beast clutched triumphantly in his hand, "I will not go."

The creature hisses angrily, but curls away from the mighty warrior and vanishes back into the depths of the arctic sea, there to remain until the twilight of the gods where he may wage his final battle. Three strikes against mortal man - the serpent is bound by vow to offer only three strikes to slay his foes. All three strikes did Diarmuid withstand, and thus the monster is vanquished.

The venom burns the flesh of Diarmuid's hand, but he notices it not. He watches the darkness dwindle over the sea of ice, and he turns, and he runs. He runs past the Sami, who watch in amazement at this swift warrior who so bested the great Jormungandr. He runs through the land of Everwinter, watching the ice melt, and the snows fade, and the slow blossoming that heralds Ostara in the valleys and hills of Eire. He runs without stopping for many days and as many nights, until finally he crosses the threshold of Qimmirea's sacred oratory. And before her wondering eyes he lays the bloody, envenomed fang of Jormungandr.

And then he faints.

—

"Diarmuid. Diarmuid, wake."

He is warm, wrapped in furs. From a window, charming light and the scents of fresh grass baking in the sun ease him softly into consciousness. He blinks.

"That's more like it." Her voice is warmer than the day. He smiles.

"Miri." His voice was low, but clear. His hand sought hers, and she grasped it tightly, weaving her fingers with his own.

"Yes, I'm here. Not out burning on some plague-damned pyre, nor wasting away in my final moments. I told you, I'm rather good at this."

He could hear the smile, the sound of relief, in the playfulness of her voice. "Is this... supposed to be a hint?"

"What? That I'm mad at you for risking your life yet again on some fool's errand for a cure that may or may not have even existed?"

"Did it... work?"

"The cheek. Of course it worked. You actually brought me the venom of the great serpent Jormungandr, the beast who marks the beginning and the end. It worked like tipping the contents of the ocean on a candle might snuff out its flame."

He laughed quietly. Through his still half-closed eyes he could see the playful grin on her own face. She still held tightly to his hand.

"Then you don't get to be... mad at me. I'm a hero." He insisted.

"Ah yes, and they'll be calling you the miracle worker next. Coming to you for all manner of cures and charms for warts, and I'll be kicked to the curbside, sent to warm my worthless bones in the icy waters of the Fyroe."

"I did it for you."

"Now that is a lie if ever I've heard one, Diarmuid, and lying is still a sin in the eyes of the Lady. You may not have done it for glory, and certainly not of the kindness of your heart, but we both know you didn't do it for me either."

"What matters if I sin," he grumbled regretfully. "The Lady still has yet to call me." *And you have yet to believe me.*

"I think she's a little busy," she replied mournfully, staring out the window at the lively spring blooming over the shadow of that deathly winter. "We lost so many, though we were not so hard hit as some of the other towns who didn't think to send their healthy into the woods. One in five of us have passed along to Tir na nOg," and she couldn't quite keep the choke of tears from her voice. "A thousand strong to swell the hosts of the dead, to join the gods in the life beyond. It is an ill omen, and a time from which I know not how we shall recover."

They both grew silent, as though to listen for the mournful call of their brethren who passed beyond the veil. They heard only the insistent sounds of spring, new life that sprang up from the ashes the hardiness of men knowing no challenge too great to be overcome.

"Miri. The child."

"Diarmuid? Your namesake? He is hale, hearty and healthy. As fair as his mother, and bids well to join the ranks of warriors from which his father hails."

"Miri..." Diarmuid sighed with a frown. She slapped his arm in jest.

"I didn't mean you, you prideful peacock. His father, we have learned, is Kivan. Surely even you would recognize Kivan's claim to their ranks?"

"I do." He winced in memory of the blighted warrior, who alone remained on the mystical isle of Cait Neth. Then he looked at her, peace stealing into his soul at the sight of the dappled light through the trees playing on her face, the softness of the curves that filled her woolen kirtle, the twilight hues that deepened the brightness of her eyes.

He was home. And so was she.

XIV

THE PURSUIT OF GRAINNE AND DIARMUID

The scent of battle and anger lingered in the air; an uncommon stench for the normally quiet graveyard. Diarmuid knitted his brows as he picked his way up the road, carefully avoiding the uncharacteristic clutter as he approached the oratory.

"What are all these stones littering the pathway?" He remarked, as he finally caught sight of Miri sitting on a gravestone. She stared blankly ahead, as though struggling to fix upon him as he approached.

He noticed dried blood from a mark on her forehead. Her eyes were unfocused. "Umm. Some folk who were... not happy."

He caught her before she collapsed. They could hear him shouting for help from leagues away.

"I'm sorry, Diarmuid. She told us she were fine; she wouldna let me touch her wound."

Aisla softly sponged away the dried blood from Miri's

forehead, leaning over her and wringing the cloth into a bowl of water mixed with herbs. Miri breathed shallowly, but the warrior couldn't tell if it was from pain or from some sort of self-induced stasis.

"What happened?" He asked hoarsely.

"Men. They called themselves the... Fianna. We sent our own up to investigate what they wanted, and the result... it wasna pretty. You should see some of the villagers."

Images flashed in Diarmuid's eyes, and Aisla thought for a moment their blue hue had taken on a reddish cast. But she blinked, and the expression was gone.

"You know of them?" She asked shrewdly. "The Fianna? I've heard tell of them in myths, but never knew them to be real."

"I do."

His brief answer gave her pause, but she waited in vain for him to elaborate. "We wondered. They asked of you. That's why they came here first. They said they sought a traitor who hid behind the skirts of a false priestess."

"A what?"

The wood creaked from the strength of his grip, and the bowl of water trembled on the table.

"That's what Fenian told me. They didn't take to it any more kindly than ye do. Qimmirea is the best of us, whether we tell it to her face or no." Aisla looked self conscious, as though she knew she were guilty of not valuing her priestess as she ought. "And then, when they caught wind of who they meant as a traitor, well..."

Her green eyes sought his. "Our menfolk liked that not. You've earned yourself a name among the Eillear. Saved us from more than the strength we muster ever could. An attack on you is an attack on all of us who welcome you into our hearts and homes."

He bowed, as much in appreciation as to hide the pain clear in the lines on his face. "I honor you, Aisla, and I honor your people. But Mi- Qimmirea. When the Fianna said such, what did she do?"

"The men said she marched inside and drew out a wand. They said she waved the wand above her head, her arms streaming bright with fresh blood."

"And then?"

Aisla swallowed. "None are quite sure. Some say the Fianna thought she were cursing them, and struck her down before she could. Others said she collapsed from weakness - they were the ones who saw her blood. But all agree the Fianna moved as though to attack. So the menfolk hailed them with curses and stones, driving the warriors from the graveyard."

Miri mumbled something in her stupor, but a raven on the windowsill cawed loudly and neither heard what she said.

"Thank you, Aisla. I can care for her from here. Go back to the village and tell them their defense of me means more than I can ever repay."

Aisla bowed, and turned to leave. Before stepping through the doorway, she paused.

"She wouldna have me as an apprentice, you know. Even when Gewinna begged on her knees. She said the Morrigan saved me not from the death brought upon my family to waste away like her as a village hedge witch. She said my duty to the Morrigan was to the family I shall raise, and that my future lay in the strength of my husband and the number of my children."

She looked long at the figure that lay still, breathing softly, on the couch. "I used to resent her for that. But I don't anymore. Goodbye, Diarmuid. Watch well over her."

—

He speaks to her silent, sleeping form. His head is bowed. The room, but for a single wavering candle, grows dark. Outside all is calm; he can hear the noises of the villagers as they feast in the long hall, breaking bread at the end of a long day.

"I did not always belong to the Fianna. But I always knew them to be the greatest of men. The most valiant of warriors, their blood and the blood of their forefathers that of the old gods. The Fianna; our Lady's Hunters."

Many and long are the legends of these fearsome warriors. They owed allegiance to no land, to no king or queen, paid homage to no vassal. They fought, and they bled, and they died, for the honor and the glory of the Morrigan. Her Lady's Hunters meted vengeance for slights against the goddess and brought before her those who, through trickery or cunning or dark magic, escaped the pull of her commanding call.

"They slew my master, the great smith Jorgeir. He had boasted greatly of his skill and of his weapons. Boasted of

their power to sunder men from their souls, their might
in the hands of a warrior to defeat even the strongest
foe. His boasts challenged the Morrigan, challenged her
right to claim those who she deemed fit to call. And so
they came for him, and over his own anvil they beheaded
him. At first, I thought he deserved it," and Diarmuid's
fists clenched in memory of claims that rang hollow, of
credit stolen by the master for work of the apprentice.
"And as I grew to know the Morrigan, and love her under
the auspices of these, her most devoted men, I began to
hate him for defying her. I grew convinced that for every
man my blade fell upon I drew closer to her. For every
sentence I passed in judgment, it was in pursuit of her
glory and her rule above all. And that..."

He drew a breath, remembering the eyes that begged for
mercy and the men with whom he rode - who, though
honorable and just in their way, were but men, mortal
men, and not gods.

"One day I realized they didn't speak for the goddess
so much as they spoke for themselves. They thought
themselves above the law they so diligently enforced.
And I felt lost. Who was I, this arrogant fool, to think
myself better than the Morrigan's most devoted
followers? But my conviction persisted with every stroke
of my sword. I could no longer kill on their orders, I
could no longer value my own life above the lives of
those I slew. I begged the goddess to call for me. I did
all I could to deserve that call. I left the Fianna, I chased
down monsters, I chased down evil men. For a while they
pursued me, and it wasn't until I was brought here," he
swallowed, putting a hand to the scar on his stomach,
"that I ever for a moment thought myself safe from them.
But I brought their danger on you."

He smoothed her hair from her forehead. She clenched

her jaw in her sleep, but other than that, she seemed composed, and comfortable. The wound on her head, sewn shut by Aisla's steady hand, brought tears to his eyes. He bit his lip and buried his head in his arms.

"Are you about to tell me you're going to leave, to protect me?"

He looked up, startled. She smiled, her eyes still closed.

"Go on, you can ask the obvious question."

His lip twitched. His dramatic ire deflated in a single moment, and he decided to humor her over pursuing his own self debasement. "How are you feeling?"

"Hmm. Not particularly great," she responded. "Aisla's a lovely girl, but her skill with a needle could stand to improve."

She shifted slightly, wincing. Diarmuid lifted her gently and propped a pillow under her shoulders. He tried to smile at her levity, but found it difficult as the weight of guilt mounted. It was his fault they attacked her, his fault they brought their violence and their accusations to her doorstep.

She sensed his discomfort. "Diarmuid. Do you think me a false priestess?"

The question was bald. But the warrior felt peace begin to steal into his heart despite himself. The quiet before the battle, the time his Lady's call, were it to come, could be heard most clearly.

"No. I don't, Miri."

She smiled, with that little crinkle on the bridge of her nose that showed she meant it. "That's why you're here. This is not the first time I've met the Fianna. Their fathers, and their fathers' fathers, were far more respectful." She got a faraway look in her eyes, and again was Diarmuid reminded of just how old she really was. "But where there are gods, there are men who think they can speak for them. We seek to draw from power that none can truly understand; we think it makes us greater than we are. Greater than our neighbors, and so able to rule them. I do not wish to rule these people. I do not wish to take the Morrigan's power and make it my own. And that is why they call me false."

She lifted his shirt, and stroked the scar across his stomach. He sighed at her touch, putting his hand over hers. "You thought once, in desperation, that you could make her power yours. You still do not know what that means. But there is innocence in ignorance, and that very innocence is why she saved you. When finally you are ready, ready to learn the truth, she will call upon you. And none, no man, no beast," her eyes flashed fire, and he realized with a start why her wand lay so long untouched above the mantle piece, "will call you before then."

He remembered Aisla's words and the way she looked at the priestess; with sorrow, and very human pity. Miri had never lived as a woman should, living instead forever alone with the ancient beings who gave her purpose and who lost hold on this growing world with every passing day. He understood with absolute clarity the draw the Morrigan's call had for this woman, abandoned on the bridge between the mortal and the eternal world and never quite belonging to either.

"Don't pity me, Diarmuid. I hold my goddess no grudge. After all, she brought me you."

He kissed her, urgently and softly. As she drew back
and sighed she saw his eyes begging for that same
forgiveness, the same humble look that stared out of the
warrior's white face when she'd stitched the wound in his
stomach together all that time ago. She stroked his cheek
with her thumb and drew his face towards her again.

There is magic in her touch, in her soul. As he drinks her
in he feels it course in his veins and soothe the fever in
his blood. Twining his fingers in her hair he presses his
body against hers, begging instead for a different sort of
blessing. She consents with a sigh and a playful nibble
at his collarbone and suddenly they are naked together,
twined in ecstasy and the most sacred of prayers.

When he slips inside her he hears a whisper of a song,
that longing filling every inch of him as he strives to fill
every inch of her. He thrusts again and again to hear her
sing, dances between her legs and surrounds himself
by the circle of her arms in simple joy. Deeper than his
longing for death rests the tranquility of his longing
for her, the softness inside her belied by the steel of her
unwavering conviction. Were he not a true hero, he
knows, he could not love her like this. As he bites at her
shoulder, and sucks at her breast, and bruises the flesh of
this holy priestess with the pressure of his lips he knows
without knowing that the Morrigan has honored her
champion with the highest of blessings.

And her magic weaves through him. As she moans his
name in his ear and bucks to meet his every stroke he
can almost see the glow of her aura and the uncanny
communion she holds with the spirits that no other
human can see. As she pushes him back against the
blankets to mount him with purpose he sees not a mortal
woman, flesh and bone, but a shining spirit with flowing

locks of fire and eyes that see beyond the veil. He grips the round hips that are clenched around his to steady her as she sways and rocks, drawing him as deep as she can into herself. As her voice begins to pitch higher, he touches the cleft between her legs to feel her shudder and nearly loses himself.

So long as he can make her move like this, cry like this, plead with the goddess and become her avatar on Eire in a single passionate drawn out moment of elaborate ecstasy, he knows he has not lived in vain.

And as her breathing slows, and he holds her collapsed and shivering form against his for just a moment longer, he knows she does not need to forgive him.

—

He knew in an instant they had returned. Their winding horns and stamping mounts; the creak and clatter of leather armor studded with iron and the clashing of axes, spears, knives and bows.

"Your friends are back," sighed Qimmirea with a grimace. "You'd think they'd take the hint."

"They've come for vengeance," he shrugged in response, but she could see the tension in his shoulders, and the fear on his brow. "I owe them that much."

"You owe nothing to no one, Diarmuid," she said, snapping her fingers and drawing down her wand again. "There are rules and laws of honor that bind us, but that which binds you is held by no mortal."

They rode swiftly up the path, stopping to dismount at the gate before the graveyard. The band had grown this time. Miri seemed pleased by this.

"Huh. So even Fionn deigns to alight from his high horse to speak with the lowly hedge witch," she murmured under her breath.

Diarmuid had gone white as a sheet. He too recognized the silver hair surrounded as it was by a circlet of bronze; the hawk-like nose and black eyes that crackled like thunderclouds.

"Miri… you don't have to…" he trailed off at the eyebrow raised in challenge at his suggestion. "Actually, forgive me. This is your house, you possess the power to grant or deny him entry."

Her charmed and conciliatory expression made him blush. "You're right I do. But I'm not about to send you off to the kitchen while we fight over you like children over a stray pup."

She watched from the doorway with arms crossed, drops of blood pooling at her feet as she gripped the rowan wand. Fionn noticed her standing there and held up his hands in peace.

"Hail, Qimmirea," he said gravely, dismounting and bowing to the priestess.

"Hail yourself, Fionn," her voice was low, and in it the growl of a cat ready to pounce. "You know the truth of this warrior as well as I and yet here you still are. What words whisper the goddess in your ear that she deigns not to whisper in mine?"

He throws back his shoulders. "It is by the goddess we have come," he insisted. "The slight upon our honor is too great to ignore."

"The man may have sworn fealty to you, Fionn," she admonished lightly, "but there is a calling greater than that of any man. You know this as well as I."

He frowned, and for a moment was silent. But at the sight of the blood dripping in the dust at her feet, he relented, putting up his hands in peace. "Release thy wand, witch. I will harm ye not. We have come to seek vengeance, it is true... but I have also come to apologize."

"Apologize?" interrupted Diarmuid, bristling. "You've a lot more to do than that."

"Silence, boy," Fionn replied forbiddingly. He turned back to Qimmirea. "Never should you have been harmed, nor any aspersions cast on your calling to the Morrigan. For that, I am most humbly sorry, and beseech your forgiveness."

He knelt before Miri, who rolled her eyes and smiled. "Are you quite done with all this formality, Fionn?" she said, while gently placing the wand on the threshold and holding out her hands for Fionn to grasp.

"Not quite," he said, turning a stern look on Diarmuid. "But we know well the futility of facing he who has not yet heard the call."

He turned to the warriors of death who ranged before the oratory, upon the backs of stamping mounts and holding each a spear or sword that knew well how to draw blood.

"Only one may challenge Diarmuid. Only one may restore the honor of our tribe. We will not all fight to die at the feet of Morrigan," and he cast a very strange, almost fearful look at Qimmirea as he spoke, "nor wet the Earth of her homely dwelling with too much of our fabled blood. Diarmuid!" He commanded, "do you accept this challenge? Do battle with but one champion, who will mete out judgement for your crimes?"

Diarmuid replied not with words. But he clutched his spear and threw from his fingers a ring, which bore the knot of Eire - a fine silver piece that showed well the skill of its artisan. It landed in the center of the graveyard, glittering among the dust and headstones.

"This ring you plucked from my dead master's finger. With this ring I pledged my allegiance to the Fianna. Defeat me, and force upon my hand this ring once more," he drew a breath, though his voice remained steady, "and I... will beg forgiveness from you, Fionn, and pledge my spear anew to your ranks. If you fail, you take this ring," and his eyes flashed fire, "and leave this place, and haunt me not any longer."

The knot of warriors grew deathly quiet. But Fionn watched for a moment and in his eyes Diarmuid saw not ire, and not fear, but something more akin to pride. He did not trust the expression, but clutched his spear all the tighter and stood all the straighter.

"One champion. Defeat this champion, and we take your ring, and your pledge, and never your doorway shall we darken again. I call not upon my warriors to pick amongst themselves who will bear their spear against yours. The goddess has long chosen your opponent, Diarmuid. Mark well upon her," and as a single warrior dismounted, approaching the clearing before Diarmuid, the blood drained from Miri's face, "for she has long sought you, and if any can bring you home it is she."

The warrior removed her helm, revealing a proud and stern face bound by braids of raven black. The strength of her jaw and the powerful lines of her body beneath her armor did nothing to mar the beauty and grace with which she approached. And beside her brown eyes - so light as to appear almost gold - drawing the attention of all, bloomed a small and rose shaped mark; a love spot. Diarmuid swallowed, and though his face remained impassive his heart quickened within him.

"Grainne," he said quietly, and bowed his head to the warrior.

"Is that all you have to say to me?" She hissed, refusing in turn to bow to him. He sighed.

"Yes. Are you accepting the role that Fionn has called for? Will you meet me in battle to weigh my guilt?" He asked, his eyes fixed on hers, in which the pain of his abandonment could still be seen.

She did not answer, but tightened her grip on her own spear. He exhaled slowly, his mouth set in a grim line.

"You do not get to mete out your own punishment, Grainne," he insisted, "for the *geas* you put upon me nor the oaths we neither of us had the authority to make."

"So that's what you think this is?" Her voice trembled, but in it he could sense the edge of her thwarted pride that muddied the waters of her grief and her anger. "I made that oath to you in earnest, Diarmuid of the Fianna, whether you honor that truth or not."

"There is only one Lady I serve, as do all the Fianna," he insisted, straightening and pressing the butt of his spear into the earth. "Now answer me and delay this not. Are you the judge for the crime levied against me by the man we called our leader?"

She bit her lip, saying nothing. But then she bowed, swiftly but gracefully, and raised her spear.

They met in a fury, the flurry of their battle sounding like an army at war though it featured only they two. The sharp crack of their spears striking one another, the gasping breath and grunts as they dodged one another's thrusts and collided in an effort to get within the guard of the other and the grit of the gravel as it ground under their leather boots. The deadly beauty of their dance bore testimony to the might and the strength of the warriors who called themselves the Lady's Hunters; the greatest in all of Eire.

As they grappled, he felt the sharp bite of metal against his palm. She held the ring and with all her strength she tried to slip it upon his finger. For a moment he froze, looking into her amber eyes, mesmerized by the spot that bloomed on her high cheekbone. For a moment the ring hovered at the tip of his finger.

But only for a moment. He regarded her sadly, knowing the depths of her pain. But he could not defy his fate to grant what she wished for hers.

"I'm sorry, Grainne," he spoke sincerely, and then with a single quick move grabbed the ring and crushed it to dust within his palm.

"I will pursue you unto the ends of this Earth!" She shrieked, with blood running through her midnight locks.

"I'm sorry it has to be like this, Grainne, I-"

She screamed and lunged at his throat with her bare hands. In an instant, Fionn and Miri were beside them, Fionn pinning Grainne's arms to her side and Miri, face twisted ferociously, raising her wand.

At the sight of her Grainne bit back a bitter, mocking laugh. Then with a twist she broke free of Fionn's grip and took off into the forest, shouldering past the rest of the Fianna who watched her in bemusement.

"Let her go," commanded Fionn, as some of the warriors turned as if to follow her. "She will return. I must ask, Qimmirea," he said, turning back towards the priestess, "that you help us find room and board amongst the villagers, for I'm afeared we left them last in a fairly... inhospitable mood."

Casting another long look at the forest into which Grainne had disappeared, Miri pursed her lips before twisting them into a smile. "I will speak with Fenian. In the meantime, make yourselves at home here," she said, sweeping past the threshold to lay her wand above the mantle again. With a ceremonious bow, she gestured them inside. "I welcome you to the hall of the priestess of the Morrigan, faithful hunters of the Fianna."

That night they gathered in Eillear's long hall. From its board they ate and drank, and shared tales of the might and the glory of the Fianna amid the starry eyed rapture of the village folk who'd heartily forgiven them for past transgressions in exchange for the honor of their presence and their stories.

"Is it true ye bury a warrior who wishes to be Fianna up to his waist, and make 'im fight the rest o' them with a shield and a spear?" cried one lad, standing up on one of the long wooden benches and waving his trencher for attention.

Fionn laughed and cast a merry glance at Conan. The red haired warrior stood and rested a knee upon the edge of the bench.

"Aye, 'tis true, child," Conan said, eyes alight in memory of his own initiation into this fair band of brethren. "On'y, am so tall, they didnae bury me deep enow. Weren't up to my waist I were buried, but my knees!" He cackled, slapping the top of one that did, indeed, seem to stretch half again the length of a normal man's leg.

Goll, a rough and wild looking warrior with wiry black hair and brows to match, elbowed his kinsman and rolled his fierce black eyes. "Yer height didnae do ye no favors when we were trapped by the fae, now, did it?"

Conan threw back his head and laughed heartily, his ears turning red as his hair.

"Nay," Goll continued, swirling the horn full of mead and leaning back against the thatched wall. "Ye were stuck in that burrow as it shrank down from the hall of gold and marble as it appeared, and we near had to chop those long legs of yours down to get ye low enough to fit out the threshold."

"Oh, 'tis fae tales we're telling, then?" scoffed Conan, with a beady look at Oisin, the golden haired warrior seated next to his father Fionn. "Remember when Oisin tried to ride a horse to the land of Tir na nOg, because a fae claimed to bless it with the power to run upon water?"

"And Grainne and Diarmuid had ter bring me back," he sighed, flicking his wrist idly, with a roll of his eyes as though he'd heard the tale too many times before.

"Outrunning my steed afore I leapt into the Firth and became one with the sea's salty spray."

Diarmuid chuckled at Miri's wondering expression. Her eyes were alight with both joy at the tales and the brightness of the fire as it burned in the center of the hall. The dim smoky atmosphere entranced them all, brought forth the otherworldly splendor of the men's tales. He could see she knew them all, had spoken them before to generations of men and women of Eire just as the priestess who lived before had taught her to do.

The cycle turns anew, he thinks to himself. *How long will these tales last? Who will tell them to our children, when we are dead and gone?*

As the firelight flickered on her rosy cheeks and in her ruddy hair, he found it hard to imagine that face lifeless, buried in a cairn beside the river. He shuddered, then wondered at himself, for the promise of death had been ever sweet. And yet now he looked upon it with something akin to dread, or the dissatisfaction of not having completed that which he was set out to do.

It is not enough that he seeks the Morrigan. He must become the kind of warrior worthy of her call. That worthiness must stem from his own conviction, but he has spent so long hoping and waiting to hear hers. As he looks into the eyes of the priestess, those indigo orbs that, like a mirror, reflect the faith and pride she had in him, he knows she could not see such value if he did not possess it within himself.

He followed her back to the oratory, leaving the Fianna to slumber in the long hall. She lingered long at the threshold of the small stone hut, staring into the forest where disappeared the thwarted Grainne.

"I had known her for as long as she lived among the Fianna," he said, following her train of thoughts and leaning in kind on the doorframe. "It seems she, much like you, had found the idea of arranged marriage distasteful. On her wedding night, she escaped in the darkness, throwing herself at Fionn's feet, desperate to escape her sordid fate. And she met every challenge he threw at her," he added fairly, "just as we all did."

"Is it true they make you run through the forest barefoot?" She replied, still staring at the ancient trees.

"Yes," he smiled. "The Fianna must be able to pluck a thorn from their heel at full stride."

"Can you still do it?"

He laughed. "Remember when I came home from the fae with a broken shoulder?"

"Yes, I absolutely do remember that."

He sucked in air between his teeth in a grimace, and she cackled.

"I guess that means you can't still do it."

"Well, I sure couldn't that time."

They fell silent for a moment, listening to the sounds of night as they echoed through the Eillear valley. A calm, quiet peace before the rising battle; the time when his goddess, were she to call, could be heard most clearly.

"I know not when the wheel turns," she whispers, as if in a trance. "I only know that turn, it does. There is a time of life, a time of death. A time of rebirth. And a time of change."

He wraps his arms around her, burying his face in her hair. She smells of victory. She smells of home.

"If it is rebirth I have found," he whispered, "then I can only be so glad I found it here."

"You speak in earnest, Diarmuid, but your actions belie your words," Miri admonished. She disentangled herself from his embrace to hold her hands out toward the moon, and its glow lit the wounds on her arm. Raw and fresh, and yet scarred over and healed by time.

"Do you know yet what it is you seek, warrior?" She whispers. "When our world does not know us, will we know ourselves?"

A waft of incense carries itself on the midnight breeze. Around him he sees the magic of Eire, the glowing lights of faerie folk, the thin strands of golden flax that weave the leylines of fate. They wind themselves around her ivory fingers, and in them he sees the glory of the past and the uncertainty of the future.

Our time is short. We make our mark and we carry it with us into the beyond. Your time is now, hero of the Morrigan. Make it count.

XV

HOLY PRIESTS OF

BJIRTKA

It is a long journey. He does not know how far he has traveled. He passes faces, forests, rivers, farms. At one point he wakes in a stone circle, eerie mists passing in and among the pale towers. At another he finds himself eating handfuls of berries he's stripped from the bushes. The road becomes a path, and the path becomes a trail, and the trail becomes nothing but that in his heart which pulls him homeward. There is a horse, and there is a cart full of hay, and at one point even there is a ship; a strange contraption of rigging and sails, and oars below deck that are barely used. For once he is seasick. And then he is angry. The gods are silent, silent, as they ever were. He wonders if they had ever even existed at all. Even when he knows, as his tired feet feel beneath them the sandy shores of Eire and his icy blue eyes see Eire's bright azure sky arching overhead and his nose fills with the smells of its sheep and its forests and its rich peat, that he is home. Even then, he wonders whether they were ever part of the magic of this land or if it had been a dream, and he has done nothing but wander forever.

And then he returns from the wide world to a home he no longer recognizes. The oratory a crumbled ruin amidst a copse of ancient trees. A stone marker that bears a name - *Qimmirea*. Effaced by time, surrounded by a ring of white lilies. He kneels beside it, strokes it with a hand he does not recognize. It is aged, wrinkled, with deep scars in its paper thin skin.

"Is it time yet, o Lady, who calls home her warriors from the battlefield?" He whispers up into the emerald screen between him and the twilight sky.

In this dream, she is the most beautiful thing he's ever seen. He can hardly look directly at her for her overwhelming glory. Her flowing black hair, with the ravens ever swirling around her noble head; he knows not where they end and she begins. Behind her, set upon a backdrop of dark stormclouds and bright ether, ranges a host of the greatest heroes of old. Their faces are stern, impassive. He wonders at that, for in life he knew them to be as joyous and hearty as children and yet here they show naught but grim respect.

Does the stamp of death hang so heavy, he thinks sadly.

"It's not what you think it is. It's never what you think it is."

Dozens of pairs of beady black eyes fix themselves upon him. He hears the chanting of the druids of old, as they sing a song of homecoming, of heartbroken mourning, hearkening to the souls of Eire's ancient champions.

"The joy you seek comes not from the arrival, but the journey itself. Have you learned this, hero? Or have you burned on the pyre of your own building, writhed on the rack of your own design?"

The ravens circle. The hush that comes in the calm before battle, the time when he hears his goddess most clearly.

"There is nothing promised beyond the moment. You are born to seek and endure. Learn to love that which you do, and not simply the result you do it for."

She speaks, but it is Miri's voice. It is Niamh's. It is the lovely druids, and Brynhilde, and Valka and Grainne and even the breathy whisper of his own mother, her eyes shining with the light of the Morrigan as she sinks onto her deathbed.

"Thig, curaidh pròiseil, tha feum agam ort."

Come, hearken warrior, to the Morrigan's call.

—

He awoke suddenly. He didn't remember sleeping but now he was awake. A hand reached out, shaking his shoulder. Aisla's face swam into view.

"Diarmuid. Diarmuid, wake."

Her voice was low, fearful almost. It roused him quickly.

"What's the matter?" He asked, peering past her through the open kitchen door. The otherwise silent oratory made him nervous. Miri, gone to Bjirtka, had yet to return.

"Come look. There's something… something wrong in Arbannen."

They climbed swiftly up the path that led to the hill crest overlooking the valley and the farthest reaches of the neighboring lands. Far, far to the east, a haze of smoke and a fiendish crimson glow lit the horizon. Diarmuid could see many of the villagers from similar vantage points, peering into the distance and gesticulating wildly.

"Who... who could have done this?"

As he spoke, he caught Aisla's eye. She was staring at a mound, a fresh grave that rose slightly higher than the earth around it, upon which a tablet and a crude wooden cross were placed.

—

"My good woman, please... Have mercy."

His eyes were wild as he knelt in the mud, and Miri felt the man's fear radiate more palpably from him than any aura. She sighed, putting a palm on her hip.

"You're not listening. This has nothing to do with whether or not I 'please' anything. I simply cannot do it. I know the land from whence you come. I know the customs you beg of me. But there is naught here for you. Draw up outside the graveyard," she insisted, slowly but firmly shutting the door, "and we will speak on the morrow."

"What of the corpse?" Diarmuid asked offhandedly. As he nailed oilcloth over the windows to keep the rain out, the shrouded figure that lay on the stones caught his eye.

"It's already dead. What will one more night do?" Miri shrugged, though he saw her hands were already busy with sewing up the shroud in which she always dressed and buried her bodies. "You know the rules. None shall cross our threshold this night, no spirit, living or dead.

He did know. He wondered at these strangers, the so-called pilgrims, who seemed ignorant of these well known ways. For at Yule, the dead of winter, to bring anyone into the home would open the door for ill luck, and danger, and mischief.

He noticed too that she slept not that night but watched, through a crack in the oilcloth, the huddled figures that crouched in the drizzling rain and prayed by the gate of the graveyard. As he rose for his morning ablutions, he heard them together in the altar place speaking in low tones. The accents of the foreigners were strange, and they stumbled over the melodious sounds that made up the language spoken by the folk of Eire.

When he returned to the kitchen, he startled the grim faced soldiers seated at the board, digging into the modest repast Miri had prepared for the travelers. One elbowed his kinsman and muttered something in a nasal and incomprehensible dialect. The kinsman chuckled under his breath, casting a disrespectful look at the warrior who stood in the doorway.

Diarmuid bristled, but before he could challenge the men to speak intelligibly or not at all Miri came into the kitchen, and gave him a look he could read all too well. He followed her wordlessly into the altar place where she sat in silence for a moment, a hand pressed to the stone idol that stood in the center of the room.

"Go down to the village. Send Aisla and Fenian to me, if you'd be so kind. I needs show these... pilgrims," she spat the foreign word with distaste, "some kind of hospitality. I cannot bury the body by myself, and perhaps if our Lord and Lady attend they'll think it meaningful enough and go away."

She seemed incredibly uncomfortable. Diarmuid hesitated at the idea of leaving her alone with these men. But she shrugged and smiled.

"They seek the holy men of Bjirtka; from what I understand, they come from the same tribe. I can only hope they mean to collect their kindred and leave Eire for good. I know they will do me no harm, I just…" Her shoulders tensed involuntarily, her brow furrowing in unease, "I speak not to their gods, and they speak not with mine."

He could sense there was more to her discomfort, and he waited patiently for her to continue. She realized this and smiled her crooked smile, though her eyes were still wary.

"The man with the tonsure, that little fat one. He won't stop praying, and he crosses himself every time he passes by the altar. He doesn't realize how well I know his tongue," she said with a ironic grimace, "nor how familiar I am already with those of his kin. Hypocrites, really. They too worship at altars, and claim they carry magical items of great power blessed by their own gods or even just the saints who act, like myself, as mouthpieces for them." She rolled her eyes, and with a hand waived the criticisms levied at her mystical trade from her mind. "But what really bothers me is the lining of his entire robe is sewn with jewels and gold."

"The foreigners are wealthy?" Diarmuid shrugged. "Perhaps they seek trade among the kingdoms of Eire?"

She rubbed her brow pensively. "The men he brought with him…" she shuddered, "They're soldiers, and they come from no army we've ever seen before. I know not what this means, Diarmuid, but I know I do not like it. They've asked me to accompany them to Bjirtka, for they struggle with our language and know not the way on their own,"

"And you will go?" replied Diarmuid, raising an eyebrow.

"Yes. But I'll be back soon, I promise. We'll sail with the merchants, and return in less than a tenday."

He knew not whether he should offer to accompany her. Her discomfort was almost tangible, but he knew better than any how capable she was. And the old warriors of Bjirtka would see that she came to no harm.

"I will bring you Fenian and Aisla as quickly as I can," he assured her, "and we'll send these less-than-merry men on their way."

The burial was quick, though the tonsured priest prayed long and mournfully over his departed kinsman. The grim faced soldiers had to go out deep into the woods to cut down a tree from which they fashioned a rough wooden cross to raise over the man's grave. By the next morning they were ready to set off for Bjirtka, sailing up the Fyroe accompanied by merchants from Eillear upon whose ship they managed to secure a berth.

He watched them sail, his eyes riveted to Miri's familiar form until they disappeared beyond the horizon.

—

Suddenly, they could see travelers on the road that led into Eillear. A huddled group that stumbled as though they'd been running for their lives and could bear to run no more. With a concerned look at one another, Aisla and Diarmuid raced for the oratory, and shortly the travelers, guided by Fenian and a small knot of concerned villagers, met them there.

"What need you, good folk?" said Diarmuid, addressing

the travelers while Aisla brought them mugs of water. "Wherefrom do you hail?"

"Arbannen," breathed one, a tall girl with honey colored curls. Her brown eyes were wild with fright, and she spoke through thin, trembling lips. Diarmuid tensed. "We... we lived in the castle. With her majesty, Queen Niamh."

At the name, two of the other travelers sniffed, burying their noses in soft cambric handkerchiefs. The men accompanying them showed no such weakness, but the depths of their eyes spoke a grief they were simply too proud to express.

"What happened to the Queen?" Aisla asked softly, resting a shaky hand on Diarmuid's shoulder. "Is she... dead?"

"Nay. But we wish... oh, my Lady, we wish she were."

Wished the Queen were dead? Aisla and Diarmuid shared an uneasy look of concern before turning back to the girl, who had dug a handkerchief from her bosom and was crying into it unabashedly.

"What mean you, lass?" Aisla asked soothingly, with a hand on the girl's shoulder.

"She be a prisoner in her own hall," she replied with a wail. "As were we all. Until..." she choked, shutting her eyes against the horrors of what she'd seen. Her next words were barely a whisper. "Those of the court who didn't manage to escape, they been executed soon after she were wed."

"Niamh is married?" Diarmuid's eyebrow rose. "To

whom?"

The girl swallowed. "P-prince Darothil," she replied shakily. "He... sir, it were most brutal. I wish not to speak of it."

She choked back a sob, and her companions shifted closer to her, sharing their handkerchiefs and their tears together. Diarmuid turned toward one of the men, a burly youth with a few wiry black bristles in his mustache and gangly limbs into which he had not quite fully grown.

"How did this happen?" He asked under his breath.

"They sacked Arbannen," stammered the youth. "Prince Darothil came with scores of men, men who wore shiny plates of armor and carried weapons of great strength. They scaled the walls and battered down the gates, then stormed the castle, slaying all within their reach."

"A handful of men took the whole castle? I understand this not," and Diarmuid shook his head with a grave look.

"Nor do we, sir," spoke another youth, his arms crossed tight against his chest. "They moved with such... practice, such accuracy. They were no novices to war, to siege. Our warriors stood no chance at all. And once they'd broke the front line they brought massive weapons to the gates, holding back our archers with heavy fire of their own. We were completely, utterly routed."

Men trained in war. Great weapons that could bear down the gates of Arbannen. What fiends had Darothil brought to Eire?

"And the Queen? What happened to her?

"Prince Darothil took his men to her tower and claimed

her as a hostage. He said he would refuse to release her until she married him."

"She spat in his face," said another, an older woman whose tears fell heavily, but in greater anger than grief. "She said she'd rather hang than share her throne with a patricide, and a usurper."

The woman's words hung heavy and sucked the breath from all who gathered in the room and heard her in disbelief.

"She accused him of patricide?" Diarmuid's eyes went wide, while Fenian and the Eillear men who accompanied them gasped, their disbelief turning to distress and fury. "How did she know this?"

"Her druids performed a ritual and spoke to Hrothgir from beyond the veil. He said that it weren't the Odin's men from the fens what murdered him, but his own son, at the behest of the holy priests."

Shock drained the blood from his face. Aisla steadied him, gripping his shoulder, while he swayed in place.

"And how... how did you learn all this?"

The older woman swallowed, and eyed him narrowly. "I was her chambermaid. She bid me to hide in the wardrobe with my children and the underservants when the raid began and men stormed the tower. I heard her every word, and I watched her as she stepped to the balustrade as if to throw herself off of it to the mercy of death on the cobblestones below. But Darothil were too quick for my lady," she sniffed, and clutched the folds of her dress in anger. "He grabbed her and threw her to the floor, and said if she tried such a thing again he would hunt down every last man, woman, and child who still lived in the palace and execute them one by one before her very eyes."

The woman went silent for a moment. In her florid face, streaked with tears, were lines of terror and agony that bloomed at the sight of her mistress, the once great and indomitable Queen of Arbannen, crushed to nothing on the floor of her own palace. He knew she would carry the weight of the Queen's surrender to her grave.

"And so she lives yet. Though for how long, we do not know." she choked back a sob, drawing a deep and watery breath.

Aisla cast a fearful look at Diarmuid, whose pale face had grown even whiter than death. "What of... the druids? You said that those who did not manage to escape were... did they find a way out?"

The woman's eyes grew fearful, and haunted. "They... they burned, my Lady. In the courtyard. They brought forth everyone they'd captured who dealt in the magics of the old gods. The druids, and the seeress from Ua Craite, and the witches they claimed defiled the land with their curses. They..." she looked around, catching sight of the wand that lay above the hearth, and shut her eyes; as though the golden spray of wheat and thin grey strands of yarn woven around it were the dancing flames and ribbons of smoke which consumed the body of its bearer. "They burned every single one. I saw them light the pyres as I fled through the city sewers."

The wood of the table creaked in protest at the strength of Diarmuid's grip. The ringing in his ears drowned out Aisla's wail of despair and disbelief.

They took her. They took her and they burned her.

He didn't speak. Aisla left the kitchen to kneel at the altar, lighting candles and chanting beseechingly, calling upon the wisdom of the gods while Fenian and the others raised their voices in ire and streamed out of the oratory to take up arms against this heinous foe. But he knew it was hopeless. The gods weren't listening. Eire had welcomed another, had let new ways in to chase out the old. He could see them, their banners against a burning sky, marching from the conquered castle of Arbannen to claim all the lands that lay surrounding it.

"Is there no hope for Arbannen, my lord?" spoke the woman fearfully, seeing the depths of despair that were clearly writ on Diarmuid's ivory brow.

He couldn't see her. Instead he was staring at a boat sailing up the river, seeing the calloused, freckled hand that waved farewell, the wrinkled bridge of the nose upon her smiling face.

There is a time of life, a time of death. A time of rebirth. And a time of change.

"You believe, like them all, that the old ways are dead," the woman, peering into his face, said mournfully. "How could we let them die?"

The beaches covered in bloody bodies, surrounded by warriors who call for victory or death. The mountains where dwell dread giants and misty forests full of fae, cunning and devilish. The aurora burning brightly over the northern seas, the chariots of the gods that once rode in Eire's night sky. The priestess, as she undresses before the altar, throwing back her head in summoning of otherworldly magics, the fire in her hair, the oil and runes on her glistening chest. The old ways always die, and new ones take their place. Sometimes in fire, and sometimes in glory.

Your time is now, hero of the Morrigan. Make it count.

He does not speak again. He simply bows to the woman, bestows a hearty shake of the boy's shoulder, and strokes the cheeks of the crying maids.

And then leaves without a backwards glance.

—

The woods resound with the echoes of wailing refugees. From Arbannen, Ua Craite, the lofty towns of Vardrfjord and Donegal and the furthest reaches of the fens to the north, the Orknyngs and Firthspit. They flee from the ceaseless march of soldiers.

"T'were her own fault," muttered a pockmarked man huddled under an oilcloth, where he sat with a knot of refugees seeking shelter from the winter rains. "If'n Queen Niamh weren't so proud and just let him be King in his own right, he ne'er would need the mercenaries to make his claim for him."

"Ye're daft, and ye're soggy," harped a wizened old woman who had her hands as close to the spluttering fire as she could get them. "Niamh wouldna honor a patricide in no way. Darothil been under the thumb o' those mealy mouthed prastes," she nodded vigorously, "and were the prastes what brought the foreign men to Eire."

Suddenly the sound of hooves drowned out their speech. In the misty gloom a man appeared, with silver hair and a circlet of bronze.

"Here now, good folk," hailed Fionn, as he drew up to the party and the rest of the Fianna fanned out behind him, "what speak you of holy priests, and foreign men?"

"Where you been then, you wraith, what you haven'a heard o' the sack of Arbannen?" grunted the woman. "Ye think we be here in yonder wretched forest fer our health? They've been razing and burning from coast to blessed coast."

Fionn grimaced, then nodded at the two warriors nearest him - the golden-eyed Grainne and golden-haired Oisin. The two dug their heels into their horses and sped off, disappearing into the forest.

"You said these were Darothil's men?" He asked, while reaching into a sack and pulling from it fresh bannocks that steamed in the chill air. Handing these to the refugees, he squatted before them and waited while they took ravenous bites.

"Aye, Prince Darothil be who led the charge. They say he been more unruly than before," answered the man, between wolffish bites of bread. "Since the plague come and sweep away so many of the old warriors, the ones what kept him knowin' he be in his father's shadow. No one ter stop him from doin' what he will. And those blasted prastes sayin' they were making him King o' all Eire if he do their bidding, or so it's said."

At this, they were once again arrested by the sound of horses approaching. Oisin and Grainne had returned.

"The soldiers come this way on foot. They've barely half a hundred leagues to go before they reach the forest," Oisin addressed his father, dismounting his horse.

"They've not yet reached the Fyroe, nor the valley of Eillear," added Grainne, who'd dismounted beside him. The woman's face was an enigma, as ever, but Fionn could sense the fear that radiated from her.

"Fionn. There are so many. I've never seen a host so strong," she added quietly. "A wave of armored men bearing plate and pikes stained with Eire's blood. They seek to drown us in it, and I know not that any have the numbers to face them."

Hushed grew the forest, even to the mist among the gnarled trees. Silence fell like snow in the ancient wood, with the promise of spring and life anew beneath its cold blanket of death. If Fionn listened closely he could almost hear a keening cry, and the march of iron boots on broken earth, and the whisper of a man's soul as it is called forth from his mortal body.

Fionn had seen many battles. He'd fallen in some, though from most, emerged victorious. He felt the ache of the spear that passed through his gut, and the pinch of the knife that slit his throat, and the heat of the fangs that crushed his ribcage. All this the man had faced and more. And endured, to live on beyond what life normally calls of its mortal beings.

But he could almost hear, in this eerie silence, the Morrigan's fateful call.

"Grainne. You said Eillear stands?"

She nodded, and from the set of her brow he knew she meant that the warrior of Eillear still stood as well.

"They will not leave the valley untouched for long. When

they turn to march upon it we must be there to meet them. My brothers, my sisters, my faithful Fianna," he sang, throwing his arms wide - knowing that though he marches to the tune of the Goddess of Death, and Chooser of the slain in battle, he does not march alone - "Are we ready to be the host which bears down this mighty foe? Will we stand beside our kin and fight, and die, for the land we love best?"

The echoes of their resounding cry carried throughout the forest, shaking the dead limbs of naked trees, rustling the feathers of birds who watched from on high, shaking the very earth upon which they stood. Even the refugees, these plain men and somber women for whom the ardor of battle never kindled, took up the cheer. These were their warriors, their champions, the greatest heroes in all of Eire. And they stood as a final bastion of the beautiful old ways of this beloved country.

For less than a hundred leagues away marched an army, an army determined to conquer, an army that promised death.

XVI

AN END

The sun has set in fire and blood. Can there be a calling greater than the salvation of one's homeland? Could any mortal withstand such a call, though it may draw the air from their lungs, the light from their eyes, the blood from their heart?

Upon the ridge there rose a legion. They bore a crest on their plated armor, a single red rose atop a black cross. They raised their shields, they raised their swords, they raised their voices in a battle cry that echoed throughout the valley of Eillear.

We have reached this far, they say, *we have found this land and will now make it ours.*

He knew he would fall that day, with a clarity he had never felt before. He saw the stakes upon which the witches had burned. The old ways would go, and he would not live to see if they went in glory or in flames.

For a moment, just one moment Diarmuid considered walking away. The enemy force was too great, too well organized. Well equipped and prepared to cut down any heathen who stood in their path. These were not raiders content for mere spoils, they wanted neither women, livestock, nor plunder. They had come for conquest. He was one man, one ember smoldering stubbornly upon an already drenched pyre.

He could be caught upon the wind, fly as far as he could, hope to set upon a plain far from their reach.

No.

And then it rose, over and through the din of the foreign battalion come to stamp them out. A song he had never heard reverberating from the earth, following the wind, reaching out from deep within the wood and the emerald hills of his homeland. A dirge unfamiliar to his ears, yet one he knew in an instant. He had waited for so long, gone to such great lengths, only to find her voice now that he'd stopped seeking it so desperately. The melody swelled in him, his body shivered as warmth coursed through his veins. He was overcome by the calm of it. The way it resonated in his heart brought tears to his eyes. *She* had taught him to live unashamed of such things, just as she had taught him the value of the life he knew he would forfeit today.

Not forfeit, no.

This was not the end of him, though it might be the end of all that he had known. Life, death, rebirth, change. She was all of these, the great and never-ending cycle that he was but a part of. The *geas* had long been lifted from his life, but there at last he opened his eyes and looked upon it in its fullness.

"Are you afraid?"

The voice was quiet, gentle. He breathed deeply and inhaled her scent. Strange that he knew it already. He dared not turn to look upon her, but her fingers laced in his left hand even as he tightened his grip on the spear in his right.

"I know you are not," she cooed, tracing a finger along his jaw. It was more calloused than he might have thought, the odor of wet leather upon it.

"Go, my hero. *Imirt mo a ceol, 's e togairt dol a dhannsa.*"

And dance we shall. For Eillear. For home. *For her.*

Her name erupted from his lips; the call was everything that still mattered to him, the cry proclaiming everything that lived in his soul. She was all of it.

He didn't expect the answer to his call to emerge from behind him. The song was joined by the raucous, hearty shouting of the men of the island, men he knew. Their footfalls quick and strong, the creaking of their leather armor and clanging of armaments tell-tale. They had come, against everything he thought of them the Fianna had answered his plea. They gathered around and beside him, hollering threats and insults at the force below them and seemingly indifferent to the impossible odds ahead. Even with the full force of the roving war band they remained outnumbered at least ten-to-one.

Fine chance, as they'd reckon.

—

Through sheer strength and perseverance, they'd managed to fracture the advancing army into three fronts. Holding out against the enemy force, even reduced as it was, still took every ounce of martial might afforded to the Fianna and the villagers who knew no quarter, only death before conquest. But for every soldier they slew two more rose up to take their place. And a new line of attack opened to their enemy with the fall of every man on the battlefield who bore the standard of Eire.

Fionn drew close to Diarmuid in the fray, the two warriors fighting as an army might. Their shields impenetrable, their spears and sword drawing the blood of their attackers with near supernatural prescience.

A tight formation of knights encircled the two warriors. All wore helms of steel, impassive metal cages that locked away the humanity of the soldiers that bore them. They moved in unison, with greater coordination and strategy than any Diarmuid had faced before. He recalled the circling wolves, the shapeshifters who posed so little of a challenge in comparison. Remembered their yellowed teeth, their brittle nails, their daggers of stone and bone.

Lifting a sword suddenly, a knight stepped out of the tight circle, swinging it overhead.

Like Dag Boor, thought Diarmuid as he mechanically shifted his spear to intercept the blow, *but without the chink in his armor.*

Instead of dodging around his opponent this time, though, Diarmuid stood his ground, protecting Fionn's back as he, too, faced off against more of the armored knights.

Their tempo began slowly, each soldier feeling out the strength and the flexibility of the warriors caught in their circle. The length of Diarmuid's spear, and the sturdy shield strapped to Fionn's forearm, kept them at bay.

The knight struck again overhead, then feinted low to draw Diarmuid's guard wide. Without missing a beat Diarmuid dropped his second spear to his hip, intercepting the strike aimed by the knight beside his assailant before heaving it higher to block his neck from yet another cut of the first knight's sword. As she recoiled he kicked through the cross of his two spears, grunting as his leather clad foot hit the metal breastplate. But he had caught the knight off-balance, who fell hard with a clatter of her heavy armor.

Metal screeched in his ears. But the sound echoed louder to the second knight as Diarmuid took advantage of his press to deliver a thrust of the butt of the spear to the temple of his steel helm.

Swearing, the man stepped back, grabbing the ringing helmet to readjust it. This Eiren devil had moved faster than wind, faster than sound itself! Their nasal curses echoed unintelligibly to Diarmuid, who had not yet broken from his position aside Fionn but instead pivoted with the man who swung his sword in an arc with strength enough to shatter the iron swords of the two who attacked him. And Diarmuid, pressing the butt of his spear into the ground, grunted as Fionn's sword rebounded off its shaft. Fionn used the momentum to swing wide once more, driving back the knights who meant to follow up their comrades' disadvantage.

The swordless knights had fallen to the dirt from the impact of the incredible strike. And though they watched as Diarmuid planted his spear with enough strength to withstand Fionn's strike they could not move fast enough to dodge as he whipped the other over his shoulder and jabbed with one strike, then two, straight into their throats.

Though the two fell easily, almost too easily, the remaining knights were undeterred. Those that Fionn had merely driven back approached again, shields high and swords higher. And the first that challenged Diarmuid, too, had regained her balance, advancing with greater caution towards this whirlwind of a warrior.

"I didn't think you still knew that trick," chuckled Fionn under his breath as he parried strikes from the knights almost lazily. Though three had beset him his shield moved too quickly, and his arm held it with such strength, that they could not break his defense. And as they tangled themselves in their own swords one cried out as Fionn's had found purchase first in the elbow of his armor, and then in his hip, and then through the visor of the steel helm that shrouded his face.

"If you didn't think I knew it, you wouldn't have tried it," countered Diarmuid, busy trying once more to use the weight of the amor of the knight opposing him to her disadvantage and topple her again. Another few strikes of the spear, the same pattern that drew the envenomed fang from the mouth of the great serpent Jormungandr, and she too lay in the dust, drinking of her own blood from a gaping wound in the hollow of her throat.

With a bloodcurdling yell, Fionn bashed the shield of his attacker with the hilt of his sword, delivering the strike with such strength that the knight dropped it from nerveless fingers. He followed up the strike with a curled fist, a blow directly to the knight's mailed helm.

The studded leather gauntlet cushioned Fionn's knuckles enough that he was able to deliver a second blow to follow up the first, toppling the knight and giving him an opportunity to stab his sword in the downed soldier's throat. The Fianna chieftain shook his hand, stretching the benumbed fingers before bringing his shield back to bear. But Diarmuid could tell the shield drooped, its weight too much for the weakened grip, and shifted his guard to protect the man's flank.

The two remaining knights drew back for a moment, unsure whether or not to press their clear disadvantage. Six of their comrades lay dead in a circle surrounding them, and they had waded past the corpses of countless others to reach these two seemingly invulnerable warriors. But they were not the only two left of the advancing army. More descended upon the grassy valley, heralded by volleys of arrows and rocks flung from slings and trebuchets that crested the hills surrounding them.

—

Atop stamping, snorting mounts Prince Darothil, accompanied by a black-visaged knight, had reached the ridge in time to view the battle as it reached its crescendo.

"Hmph. I thought you said the plague wiped this land of its heathens?" The knight grunted, seeing the remaining band of determined warriors that held their own against the wave of foreign soldiers.

"It seems some managed to evade death. It matters not. They cannot evade it forever, Strongbow," scoffed Darothil, shrugging his shoulders at the sight of the men below. "You hear their call to the ancient Goddess? They seek her gift this day, and your god shall be the one to grant it."

"Silence, heretic," spat Strongbow, the great Knight of Strigul, who had chosen to descend upon Eire in a holy pilgrimage to wrest its people from their heathen gods and civil wars. "The plague was wrought as punishment upon those who deny our god, in his sole might and glory. He uses not the wicked usurpers of his holy title as a means to exact his will." He beckoned to the archers lined up in a row along the ridge, staring down at the pitiful bastion that made its stand against them. "They can cry to their goddess all they want. She is a lie, a pitiful lie, and one they will learn the truth of too late."

Smoke filled the air. Every single villager of Eillear that could bear arms had taken up the fight, though most, only to die against the organized and coordinated foe. The rest, knowing it futile to hope for victory, had begun to burn the village and retreat into the river. They knew they could not escape for long. They knew the inevitable could be only delayed. With pride that could little bear conquest by such foes, they burned their homes so as not to see them fall into the hands of the force that murdered their kinsmen with such wanton abandon.

Prince Darothil looked on in some confusion. "How does the village burn? Did your men manage to break through their defense somewhere? This is not what we agreed, Strigul," he contended, unwilling to lose the fertile valley and the homage of its hardy people.

"They'd rather burn their own village to the ground than watch it fall into the hands of the oppressor," remarked Strigul coldly. He did not care.

Darothil swallowed hard, but he had marked his course and meant not to sway from it. This land would be his, no matter the sacrifice, no matter the cost.

The old gods would die along with their heroes.

—

Ribbons of flame shot into the sky, challenging the dying light of the sun and flashing viciously on the shiny breastplates worn by the advancing army. No defiance could slow their march. And it seemed no muster could be brought that might possibly promise victory. Some to arrow, and some to blade - one by one their heroic militia fell to the oncoming horde. Diarmuid's momentum slowed, though he still fought mechanically even as the stench of burning reached his nostrils. He thrust his spear and drew forth the blood of his enemies, despite knowing he protected naught but ash.

Is this what I've been waiting for?

The screams of dying men and women, the grating of sword against shield, the roar of flame and pounding of armored boots.

Is this your fabled call, o Lady of Death?

This was war like he'd never seen it before. Though he had yet to die, he could hear it whispered, a promise on the wind. He could not see the light of life leave the eyes of those he faced, their visors down, blank, dispassionate. They move like automatons across the field bent upon a single purpose: domination, inevitable and swift. No matter the sacrifice, no matter the cost.

Ravens circle in the murky sky overhead. He cannot see them, but he knows they are there. He wonders if they have already shepherded the souls of the druids, the witches, the *bean feasa* who had lived so long upon this land she seemed almost a stranger to all who walked upon it with her. The hilltop oratory is obscured by smoke and dust. The ancient forest, too, shaded in impenetrable gloom.

"How long do we keep this up?" panted Diarmuid as wave after wave of soldiers crashed upon them, with sprays of blood in place of salty foam that burst above the wooden shields, standing rooted as the craggy cliffs that endured the ceaseless pounding of the sea.

"For as long as it takes," rasped the Fianna chieftain beside him. Tears tracked through the mud and gore upon his face, tears wrought from anger at the destruction brought upon Eire and wrought from pain at the sight of bodies that lay trampled upon the battlefield.

Oisin's golden hair spilled from his broken helm, mixed with the dirt upon which his lifeless form lay amid a knot of slain soldiers. He seemed almost peaceful in death, though not moments before he had fought as one frenzied, severing limbs and hewing heads from necks attached to men who thought they would never bear down such a giant. But bore him down they did.

Grainne's golden eyes fixed sightlessly upon the tightening spiral of ravens wheeling mournfully, ceaselessly, in the darkening sky above. Some perched upon the shafts of arrows embedded deep in plated armor, fired with inhuman strength from her bow before she, too, had been overwhelmed.

"They want to write us from our own tales," Fionn said through bloody lips. Sheer numbers alone had near routed the old warrior. His arm hung limp at his side, one eye closed forever, the other near blinded with blood that streamed from a wound on his brow. "We lived unto this day to deny them that pleasure. Though we die," and he looked longingly, lovingly into the beckon of the beyond, "we do not die eternal. They will sing of us, and of the land and legends we fought and died to protect. When the time comes for them," he gestured to the standard of the advancing army, the cross of black and the rose of red, "when their day dies as our own has done, those who seek their destruction will remember us. They will know a time came before, and so they will have strength to stand for a time that must come after."

For a moment he could see them. Diarmuid, as he peered through the haze of battle and the clouds of dust, saw them. The men and women of the future, marching and chanting for change against the dominance of this regime that sought to shape mankind. They fought not with sword and shield but with banners, and with words, and with volume of numbers alone. A millennia from now, in a world the warrior could not even begin to recognize, he knew that many would stand against this brutish force and demand it give way.

And they would win. They too, would die, as his kin had. But unlike them, they would win.

"We fight for their future," he whispered to himself even as he heard the inevitable volley of arrows that descended upon them, even as the war horns sounding in the hills surrounding Eillear heralded fresh troops ready to maintain the advance of the invaders. A reminder that the end of Eire was inevitable, as inevitable as the march of time. Life. Death. Rebirth. Change.

"They will remember us."

—

It was exactly as he knew it would be. Every bone in his body, every drop of his warrior's blood understood that it was hopeless from the outset. They had done as well as they could against Darothil's force, but the foreign knights and their multitude of archers could not be overcome. He inhaled heavily, with exceeding difficulty. The damage to his ribs had progressed into his lungs, piercing them, flooding his increasingly labored breath. He lay upon the ground beside Fionn, who'd fallen beside him. Blue crept upon his lips; his frenzied frame bloodied and broken in more places than he could feel any longer, let alone see through eyes hazing with dark fog.

Despite his dulled senses, his ears registered the beating of wings. His eyes caught sight of black feathers passing through his field of vision. He smiled, coughing through the drowning sensation welling in his chest.

He saw her, at last he saw her. The face of his beloved met his eyes, her calloused hands took his in them, her tears fell upon his chest. Taking blood and filth from his armor as they streamed down.

"Miri..." He sighed and lay still, his eyes drifting shut as she sang to him one last time.

He smiled.

And then, he died.

Looking For More Iron Breaker Books?

www.ironbreakerbooks.com